ENRIQUE VILA-MATAS

Montevideo

A NOVEL

Translated from the Spanish by
Sophie Hughes and Annie McDermott

A MARGELLOS
WORLD REPUBLIC OF LETTERS BOOK

Yale UNIVERSITY PRESS | NEW HAVEN & LONDON

The Margellos World Republic of Letters is dedicated to making literary works from around the globe available in English through translation. It brings to the English-speaking world the work of leading poets, novelists, essayists, philosophers, and playwrights from Europe, Latin America, Africa, Asia, and the Middle East to stimulate international discourse and creative exchange.

Published with assistance from the foundation established in memory of James Wesley Cooper of the Class of 1865, Yale College.

Yale University Press books may be purchased in quantity for educational, business, or promotional use. For information, please email sales.press@yale.edu (US office) or sales@yaleup.co.uk (UK office).

Set in Source Serif type by Motto Publishing Services.
Printed in the United States of America.

Library of Congress Control Number: 2025936026
ISBN 978-0-300-28483-6 (hardcover)

A catalogue record for this book is available from the British Library.

Authorized Representative in the EU: Easy Access System Europe, Mustamäe tee 50, 10621 Tallinn, Estonia, gpsr.requests@easproject.com

10 9 8 7 6 5 4 3 2 1

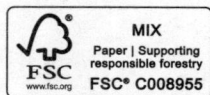

To Paula de Parma,
tiembla mi alma enamorada.

Contents

Paris

In February of '74 I traveled to Paris with the anachronistic intention of becoming a writer from the 1920s, "lost generation" style. That was my, shall we say, unusual aim on moving there, but even as a young man I couldn't fail to notice, as I wandered the streets, that Paris was absorbed in its latest revolutions, and this filled me with a vast, monumental laziness, an overwhelming lethargy at the mere thought of having to become a writer there, let alone a lion hunter à la Hemingway.

To hell with everything, especially my aspirations, I said to myself one evening as I crossed the Pont Neuf. There must be some way of escaping this fate, I'd been thinking nonstop throughout that day. In the end, I turned down a dimly lit street and embarked on a life of crime that somehow plunged me back into an adolescent mindset that I thought I'd put behind me: the classic dispirited state of a young man whose great poems would revolve around "solitude" and his "weatherworn soul," were he not too busy selling drugs to write them.

In Paris, at any rate, I wasn't so foolish as to be taken in by the total void, which had already wrecked my first youth, in Barcelona. Instead, I succumbed to a kind of controlled meaninglessness, bordering almost on pretense, and did little else but explore, in considerable depth, from top to bottom, the seedy side of Paris, the diabolical side, that glorious city described in *The Other Paris* by Lucy Sante (neighborhoods rife with flâneurs, Apaches, chanson stars, clochards, brave revolutionaries, and street artists), the Paris of outcasts, the Paris of anti-Franco exiles with their well-organized drug ring, the Paris of washed-up has-beens, the Paris of great social vertigo.

A Paris that, many years later, would be the setting for my account of those days spent dealing hash, marijuana, and cocaine, during which I failed to devote a single minute to writing, and was overcome, what's more, by a sudden indifference to culture more generally; an indifference that cost me dearly in the long run and was even reflected in the oafish title I gave to my account of those turbulent times: *A Garage of One's Own.*

Paris, for me, during that first two-year stay, was simply a place where I sold drugs and where, for a brief three-month period that went by in a flash, I was addicted to lysergic acid, LSD, which showed me that what we call "reality" is not an exact science but a pact between a great many people, a great many co-conspirators, who might one day decide, for example, that the Avenida Diagonal of your hometown is a tree-lined boulevard, when in fact, after a dose of acid, you can see quite plainly that it's a zoo teeming with beasts and tropical birds, all with a life of their own and running amok, some even swinging in the treetops.

During that first two-year stay, my Parisian world was limited to a modest patch controlled by small-time dealers and the odd party full of depressed Spanish exiles; lousy parties, albeit with plenty of red wine, and from which all I remember is the habit I developed of saying goodbye to each and every one of my pseudo-friends and acquaintances with the words:

"Did you know I've stopped writing?"

At which point someone would invariably jump in and correct me:

"You never wrote in the first place!"

And it was true, I didn't write, or rather I hadn't since back when I published my first and only book, the exercise in style I completed in some barracks in the North African city of Melilla. It was titled *Nepal* and consisted of a veiled take-down of the bourgeois family, along with an explanation of how I intended—blessed innocence, I had yet to set foot in Paris, or venture down that dimly lit street—to remain utterly unchanged, identical to my current self for as long as I lived; in other words, to remain in thrall to the wholesome hippie ways I had found so seductive until some countercultural, libertarian, pacifist scoundrels took me to work a sugar beet harvest and everything changed overnight.

No one in Paris knew, nor was there any reason why they should, that I had written and published a book on my return from Africa, a little novel that passed itself off as having been written in Kathmandu and whose prose was so experimental that the critique of the bourgeois family went entirely unnoticed. I'd never told anyone about my days in Melilla spent playing at feeling like Gary Cooper in von Sternberg's *Morocco* (though I lacked all the requisites to pull it off—Marlene Dietrich, for starters), and this gave me, among other things, the chance to try my hand at being someone else, at reinventing myself, though in the end I always found that, much as

I longed to be many different people and to have been born in many different places, my likeness to myself was just too strong, and not a day went by when I wasn't reminded that the risk of trying to be someone else is precisely that we end up resembling ourselves.

2

It was very unusual for someone in Paris not to write, I should add. Cioran described this phenomenon in a note recounting what the doorwoman in his building had said to him one day: "The French don't want to work anymore, they all want to *write.*"

"You never wrote in the first place!" people always corrected me as I walked out of parties armed with explosive quantities of wine and hash. Nonetheless, I would say goodbye in the exact same way a few days later; I relished announcing that I'd given up writing just to hear that fantastic: "You never wrote in the first place!" which I got used to pretending I hadn't in fact heard, mindful that this would allow me to reuse my parting line at other opportunities in the future.

These days it's pretty clear to me that, long before I even started to write—or rather, having written *Nepal,* which amounts to the same thing, since you couldn't call that writing, or even an exercise in style—I had an almost irresistible desire to leave writing behind, which is something I've done well never to lose sight of. In fact, that poetics of wanting to abandon the work before it became the work was what turned me, in the long run, into an expert in shifting back and forth around the wheel of the five narrative trends, though I've always thought, or rather *felt,* that there's actually a sixth, without ever managing to put my finger on it.

At one time I moved around that wheel like a madman, although I never visited the fourth category, which is reserved for God and Kafka's uncle, better known as "Madrid's uncle"—an impressive pair, for all that you never know where they might land.

I had rough rides through four of the five categories, beginning in Barcelona as a very young man, back when I was just another of those writers "with nothing to say" (narrative trend number one) and who, as such, are capable only of kicking stones down the streets of their own limitless boredom. After that, I launched into trend number two and grew very skilled at suppressing certain aspects of the stories I wrote, a strategy that reaped high returns, to the point that I became a virtuoso in writing stories that *deliberately* didn't tell the reader anything. That period paved the way to narrative trend number three, the most crowded of them all, occupied by those who like to leave a loose thread in the story they're telling and wait for God to tie it up one day, or if not God, then Kafka's uncle, these being the two sole lords and masters of narrative trend number four and legendary beings in their own right—the former more so than the latter—about whom it was always said that, in their efforts to say something sensible, they ended up saying nothing at all, as if they were enemies of any kind of eloquence. As for trend number five and the future hackers (who, to an extent, already walk among us, like Martians, and sometimes fall more broadly under the generic name of "social media"), we can only hope that in time they function exclusively as if they were part of the North American espionage system; a system which, strange as it may seem, has some points in common with the "bachelor machine" used by the brilliant Raymond Roussel to write his works.

That invention by the author of *Impressions of Africa*—a genius ahead of his time and forefather of the digital era—tirelessly pumped out language, an astonishing and unending stream of writing, which itself boasted infinite internal echoes that ensured that the "textual machine" never ground to a halt.

Around and around that wheel I went, becoming better acquainted with some trends than others, but ultimately dabbling in them all, aside from that of the enemies of eloquence, a category in which, if I'm not mistaken—because in Montevideo I did get a sneaking feeling I'd wandered a little too far into the darkness—I never set foot.

The five trends are as follows:

1. That of people who have nothing to say.
2. That of people who *deliberately* don't say anything.
3. That of people who don't say everything.
4. That of people who hope one day God will say everything, including why it's so imperfect.
5. That of people who've given in to the power of technology, which seems to be transcribing and recording everything, and rendering the writer obsolete in the process.

The first category—the only one I ventured through back in that Paris of the seventies—always sent me to a gray postwar Barcelona landscape with a solitary figure at the center of the scene, in the middle of Paseo de San Juan. A skinny, timorous, bored student: me, in other words. A solitary figure whom I associate these days with an observation Ricardo Piglia made about his youth and about the earliest years of his diaries ("Because there I wrestle with the total void: nothing happens, nothing ever happens in reality. And what could happen?") and also with the diary of Paco Monteras, my only high school friend who knew how to pretend he was having fun but who, decades later, let me read those pages, not without first warning me that they were ferociously dull—and "so *ocher*" (a term I'd never heard used that way)—with entries that offered little more to the reader than his detailed ruminations on the weather.

3

A sizable chunk of Montparnasse, and in particular the very short Rue Delambre, once home to Gauguin, Breton, and Duchamp, among so many others, was the main hub of my pseudo-commercial activities: small-scale, hard-won drug deals on the streets, selling exclusively to the punters stumbling out of either the Rosebud Bar or Hôtel Delambre. Calle del Hambre, I called it—Hunger Street—and sometimes it was even gratifying to feel I'd hit upon the perfect name for that patch where, in order to feed myself—that is, to survive—I sold anything and everything, ever conscious that, as an equally wretched Spanish friend of mine would say, the only thing a foot soldier on the battlefield has is his survival.

The Rosebud was the bar–cum–jazz club in Paris that

stayed open the latest. One day I'll come back as a customer, I'd tell myself, always trying to keep my chin up. The Rosebud had affordable prices for the professional night owls and was patronized above all by the city's most American Americans—read, if you will, its most *Hemingwayan* Americans. It's still there today, and fairly recently I was able to confirm that it hasn't changed, though now it closes earlier and you have to smoke outside, in the street. The cocktails are the same as they always were and sound like something from another era. In fact, nowadays their names would be positively archaic (Sidecars, Singapore Slings . . .) if Don Draper from *Mad Men* hadn't brought them back into fashion.

4

It made me laugh to think that I'd gone to Paris to turn into a North American from another time and had ended up selling drugs to North Americans of the here and now.

It happened not far from the Rosebud, at 25 Hunger Street, in the legendary Dingo American Bar, now the pizzeria Auberge de Venise. That night I was even more rushed off my feet than usual trying to shift the day's stock. And it was then that I came to meet a category-four militant, an "omniscient narrator" (God-style, though seemingly without God's indisputable status), a writer with designs on trend number four but whose divine airs were rather unconvincing. Always keen to throw potential snitches off the scent, I was gazing up at the sky like someone most definitely not involved in any criminal activity when along came "the omniscient one," a somewhat eccentric old man wearing sunglasses, dressed immaculately in white in the middle of winter, who asked if I was navigating by the stars. I immediately assumed he was a police informant or similar, but my fears were completely unfounded.

"Young man, you're looking at the sky to get your bearings, I can see that much, but never forget, I was the one who created the heavens," the old man said.

He wasn't drunk, which meant he could only be your typical loony grandpa. I played along and asked if he had also created the moon. "And the stars," he said. "Nothing is beyond me, and if you like I'll tell you everything."

"Everything?"

"Yes, all of Creation," he said. "Has anyone ever given you the full story of how the world was created?"

This was nothing new to me. How many people had jumped on the first chance they got to attempt to tell me everything, knowing full well that they could never cover so much as a millionth of the world's developments since at least the Paleolithic era? But of course, the world is full of pursuers of totality, some of immeasurable worth and boldness, like Herman Melville, the first person who springs to mind when I wander through the world of the pursuers of Everything. I've always thought that, with *Moby-Dick,* he created an immense metaphor for immensity, for the immensity of our ignorance.

One day, in the Bronx, as it was getting dark, in the seemingly interminable Woodlawn Cemetery, my friend Lake and I realized we were getting no closer to finding Herman Melville's grave and asked the "Cemetery Police" (consisting of two Puerto Rican law enforcement officers in a patrol car and carrying guns, almost like something out of the Wild West) where it was. After we'd unfolded our enormous map, and perhaps because they'd never heard of Melville, they somehow got the idea that we were literally looking for the grave of Moby Dick and pointed to a vast area, a vague green splotch on the map, where the famous whale had supposedly been laid to rest.

Good grief, we thought, these policemen think we're looking for the most enormous grave in here, conceivably big enough to fit the whole world. And with the pursuers of Everything still on my mind, I recalled Miklós Szentkuthy, another one suspected of wanting to encompass the absolute, a Hungarian genius who said he wanted to see, read, think, dream, and gorge himself on everything, absolutely everything. And of course, I also remembered the exorbitant Thomas Wolfe, who, in his eagerness to take in all the world's stories, drowned in the storm of those materials that seemed to evade his grasp. This eagerness of Wolfe's to rule over time could be seen in his torrential first novel, *Look Homeward, Angel,* which included some words that I've always deemed worthy of constant reflection and that could be said to form the crux of my own poetics:

> "We seek the great forgotten language, the lost lane. . . .
> Each of us is all the sums he has not counted: subtract us
> into nakedness and night again, and you shall see begin
> in Crete four thousand years ago the love that ended
> yesterday in Texas."

5

I spent last night engrossed in Werner Herzog's documentary filmed inside the Chauvet Cave in the Ardèche region, in the south of France: a Paleolithic cathedral dating back some forty thousand years, and closed to the public. I was particularly excited to watch it because, on my return from Melilla, I had spent a lot of time studying the Paleolithic era, and my interest hadn't waned over the years. Quite the contrary: my mind was positively steeped in memories of my research into that inexhaustible topic. Among them, a phrase from Georges Bataille, written in *Les larmes d'Éros,* long before Herzog's documentary, of course; a phrase introduced to me by the writer Juan Vico: "these somber caves were actually consecrated above all else to what is, at bottom, play—play as opposed to work, play whose essence is above all to obey seduction, to respond to *passion.*"

Only the archaeologists and paleontologists working on the ground to document their findings had access to the Chauvet site, which Herzog was allowed to enter by special arrangement and with a minimal film crew. Among those who went with him was Jean-Michel Geneste, a Paleolithic archaeologist whom I once had the honor of meeting and whose revelatory words at the end of the documentary I noted down, feeling that I'd been given, for the first time in my life, a highly convincing lead that might help me find what I'd spent so many years searching for: "the great forgotten language, the lost lane" of which Wolfe and so many others have spoken.

It seemed Geneste got to the heart of the "lost lane" when he remarked, at the end of the documentary, that humans from forty thousand years ago, Paleolithic humans, likely held two concepts that, when considered today, significantly change our perception of the world: *fluidity* and *permeability.* According to Geneste, *fluidity* means that the categories we deal in—woman, man, horse, tree, door—can shift and change. Just as a tree can speak, a man, given the right circumstances, can turn into an animal and vice versa.

Permeability, meanwhile, refers to the idea that there are no barriers, as it were, in the spirit world. And I can't be sure, but my feeling is that these two concepts cited by the French archaeologist would have fitted wonderfully well into Italo Calvino's *Six Memos for the Next Millennium,* which is something of a bible to me. In fact, it would have been marvelous to see how, with the addition of Geneste's two concepts, the *Six Memos* could have incorporated an ancient, more fluid and spiritual perception of our world.

Walls, Geneste tells us, can talk to us, accept or reject us. A shaman, for example, can send his spirit into the supernatural world or receive supernatural spirits within himself. If we view *fluidity* and *permeability* together, we can appreciate how vastly different life must have been back then. Humans have been given many different labels, *Homo sapiens* among them, laughably arrogant it may be as a moniker given we still don't know that the only thing we do know is that we don't know anything. *Homo spiritualis* would seem a more apt definition. For do we not faintly detect, in Werner Herzog's movie about the French Chauvet cave, the origin of the modern human soul? Last night, the sense of having almost detected it—that origin, somehow so visible inside the French cave—left me wandering down the "lost lane," the same one I sometimes make my way along, or think I do, when I feel myself being spurred onward by a voice that feeds my soul, and indeed fuels no small amount of soul-searching: "Come on, we've got a lot of ground to cover."

6

What fascinated me about Thomas Wolfe, one of the twentieth century's pioneers in speaking about that "lost lane," was his eagerness to take in everything, his tireless efforts to fix in his mind every brick and paving stone of every street he'd ever walked down, every face in every bustling crowd in every city, every town, every country, yes, and even all the books in the library whose packed shelves he had tried in vain to work his way through as a student.

As a novelist he seemed blessed with certain divine gifts, if such gifts can ever really be part of a writer's soul. The first time I read something hostile about these totalitarian authors—God's close and somewhat desperate competitors— was at a conference featuring Antonio Tabucchi, whose *The Woman of Porto Pim* I had just begun to admire; a glorious, genre-spanning book first published in Palermo and translated in Barcelona in February 1984, somehow both hodgepodge and utterly cohesive, bringing together in very few pages short stories, fragments of memoirs, diaries of metaphysical shifts, personal notes, a brief biography of Antero de Quental, snippets of a story casually overheard on a ship deck, invented memories, maps, bibliographies, abstruse legal texts, and love songs: a whole series of different elements, some on the face of it incompatible with one another, and certainly incompatible with literature, but transformed, by firm writerly resolve, into pure fiction.

What I loved about *The Woman of Porto Pim* was the highly unconventional organization of its texts, so similar in structure—at least from my point of view—to *Sleepless Nights,* another genre-spanning book of great importance, also as hodgepodge as it is cohesive, in which Elizabeth Hardwick uses fragments of memoirs and personal notes to build up the portrait of a self-made creator, who has some clear influences but is essentially unique, and always a little weary, like a Billie Holiday of literature, surrounded by musicians even more tired than her, with sunglasses, ashen insomnia, heavy overcoats, and wives, all so blond and so very exhausted.

There are pages of Hardwick that I wish I knew by heart, such as the one where she tells us that on thinking of the unfortunate people she's known, she has the impression they "live surrounded by their kind. The windows resent their curtains, the light its woven shade, the door its lock, the coffin its loathsome, suffocating pile of dirt."

One of the things I remember most clearly about *The Woman of Porto Pim* is Tabucchi's poetic lightness of touch when writing about difficult or complex matters, how in his hands they become less heavy. It's as if Tabucchi believed only levity could convey the true nature of things and that anything too ponderous would invariably blind the reader, stopping them from reading on. In his book—though, of course, without actually saying so—Tabucchi offers nothing less than a *Moby-Dick* in miniature.

I read this sweeping diminutive travel book around the time I discovered, ten years after my return from Paris, that my best friends in Barcelona had made something of their lives, while I was completely adrift in mine. And if I'm not mistaken, it was very shortly after reading *The Woman of Porto Pim* that I had a kind of epiphany and decided—to my joy and immediate, enormous sense of relief—that I would return to writing, as if that might rescue me from something, at the very least from the gloomy cellar into which I realized I had clumsily, needlessly fallen.

Something that proved providential to my efforts not to end up like those people whose windows resent their curtains was a panel discussion involving Tabucchi, reproduced in a Spanish newspaper, which I read very closely indeed. There had been a gathering of several Italian writers in Rome, during which Antonio Tabucchi had come out and said that the nineteenth-century novelist, "in his omnipresence," bore too close a resemblance to God (who was in everything, and saw everything, and was Everything), adding that this actually made him seem like some cruddy old relic from the past. "And as such, eminently crushable," quipped the entertaining Tabucchi. I laughed for days, because I couldn't stop thinking about that conclusion, or rather, that unexpected final adjective: *crushable.*

When, months later, out of sheer curiosity, I traveled to Italy to see Vecchiano and spend a few days in Rome at the jolly Albergo del Sole in the piazza at the Pantheon, I read, printed beside a soccer write-up of all things, in a newspaper I found in the reception, a line from Voltaire that took me by surprise, perhaps simply because I hadn't expected to find it in the sports section:

"The secret of being a bore is to tell everything."

It got me thinking. Soccer matches, for example, gave everything away and often weren't at all boring. Was extra time invented for matches that hadn't yet resolved the game's action?

The secret of being a bore is to tell everything, Voltaire said. But it seems the young Kafka didn't agree when, in one of his earliest texts, "Description of a Struggle," he demanded that everything, absolutely everything, be told to *him:* "And now I shouted: 'Come out with your stories! I'm done hearing scraps. Tell me everything, from beginning to end. Any less and I won't listen, I warn you. But I'm burning to hear the whole thing.'"

7

Arguing that the secret of being a bore was to tell every-thing proved, at least for me, an effective way of ostraciz-ing the nineteenth-century author and his particularly over-bearing brand of knowing-it-all. But eventually I discovered a different type of omniscient narrator who was not in the least dull, quite the contrary. Herman Melville, the author of *Moby-Dick,* for example. I wrote this observation down in a notebook and felt immediate satisfaction at having put an end to my absurd habit—which had gone on for decades—of systematically and indiscriminately snubbing nineteenth-century authors, an obsession which I realized belatedly, though just in time, I desperately needed to get over.

Putting that tired old line about the nineteenth-century writers to bed opened up new horizons, and what's more al-lowed me to try my hand at the art of rolling back and forth like a ship on the high seas, and from time to time to con-sider the marvelous variance between, for example, Tabuc-chi's miniaturized world in *The Woman of Porto Pim* and the colossal scale of Herman Melville's *Moby-Dick,* where every-thing is monumental; the whales, for a start. And where, what's more, Melville's immense encyclopedic zeal shines through undeniably and irresistibly, for instance when he tells us that the best whalers in the world used to come from the imposing Pico Island in the Azores.

Months after my trip to Vecchiano and Rome, I met Tabucchi for the first time in Barcelona at a party at the Hotel Colón, next to the cathedral. I wanted to tell him about my visit to Vecchiano, his hometown, but before I could, he suggested, without so much as glancing at me, that I accompany him to a bar on the other side of the room. We had to jostle our way through a great many people to reach the gilded bar, taking a very roundabout route. I followed Tabucchi, who cut through the jungle of drinkers with remarkable ease, as if wielding a machete. At one point on that odyssey to the other side of the room, he asked me point-blank, in an accent that was somewhere between Italian and Portuguese:

"My friend, why are you *pursuing* me?"

I understood right away what he meant by that question: he obviously knew that in one of my newspaper articles I'd literally copied out part of his description of Peter's Bar, a legendary joint in the Azores that I would soon visit for myself but which, even before that, thanks to *The Woman of Porto Pim,* I was able to describe as if I'd been going there all my life.

That day, as we made our way through the jungle to the bar, I pretended not to have caught the veiled reference (and presentation card of sorts) and instead told him how in Paris I'd given up writing but that afterward, back in Barcelona, I'd changed my mind and started producing stories like mad, to the point that I turned my back on real life.

You mean you turned life into literature, said Tabucchi,

because, if you think about it, the mere act of telling me that in Paris you gave up writing *is* literature, and there's no getting around that for either of us, wouldn't you say?

8

The next character I want to bring in might seem like something out of a Christmas story but in fact is very real indeed: a clochard who, every day toward the end of the last century, could be found sitting in the doorway of a bookstore in Paris, on Boulevard Saint-Germain, facing an iconic newsstand. The bookstore no longer exists, and I've heard nothing about the clochard for years; only the newsstand is still there.

That man who used to sit on the ground—the ground is also still there; I always take a quick look whenever I'm in Paris—was one of the most refined people I've ever met, and not only because of his elegant demeanor or because he bid good morning to all who paused at the newsstand or entered the bookstore, but because he spent his time reading the classics, right there on the cardboard boxes he neatly arranged on the ground and from where he would occasionally look up and contemplate the general traffic of the world. Once or twice I'd watched him suddenly get to his feet and, in the manner of Che Guevara, almost arrogant, his gaze fixed on the horizon, smoke a colossal Havana cigar that unnerved more than the odd passerby.

I'd already noticed him from time to time during my first stint in Paris, which I spent renting a small corner of a garage in the north of the capital, and these sightings continued over the years whenever I found myself back in the city. But I never imagined that one day, in Florence, the writer Antonio Tabucchi would start talking to me about that Havana-smoking clochard.

As we sat together on the summer terrace of a café beside the Arno River, Tabucchi told me he'd once entered into conversation with the man, a well-known figure on the Boulevard Saint-Germain. The scene he went on to describe took place one evening when the snow was falling heavily over Paris and Tabucchi was alone in the city and, feeling restive in his small apartment on Rue de l'Université, had decided to go out for a walk. He hadn't seen another soul in the neighborhood until he chanced upon his friend the clochard, in whom he confided his deep distress at being alive, and at the bleakness of that winter's day.

The man's only response was to invite Tabucchi to join him on the cardboard boxes spread out on the sidewalk and to observe the world from his lowly position on the ground. Tabucchi immediately accepted, and there they sat for a long while, in the doorway to the bookstore, contemplating from below the comings and goings—at times hurried, at others maundering, but always indifferent—of the winter passersby, until the clochard broke the silence to say something that Tabucchi had never forgotten:

"You see, my friend? From here it's so obvious. These men and women walking by—they're not happy."

On my return from Florence, mulling over the words of the clochard, whose name I never learned, I recalled what coeditors Augusto Monterroso and Bárbara Jacobs had said in the introduction to their 1992 *Anthology of Sad Stories:* "If it is true that a good story contains a whole life, and if it is true, as we believe it to be, that life is sad, a good story will always be a sad story."

Of course, they also said in that introduction that life's happy side sometimes has its basis in the sad side, and vice versa, which has often led me to think that the Parisian clochard also had something of a happy animal about him, in particular something of those happy whales that observe the whalers and describe what they see in a story from *The Woman of Porto Pim*. Those whales, with tragic tenderness, believe they can see that the men who approach them "soon get tired and when evening falls they lie down on the little islands that take them about and perhaps fall asleep or watch the moon. They slide silently by and you realize they are sad."

Sometimes short stories (you could see it clearly in Tabucchi's) are slices of life with a strange proximity to reality. Especially when they're told by happy people or whales, for whom sadness is a matter of life and death. "To see me die among sad memories," as Garcilaso once said.

9

Lightning strikes in Barcelona and my memory transports me back to the Marigny Theater, on the Champs-Élysées.

I had returned to that Paris of drugs and renunciations of writing some fifteen years later, and I discovered I'd made my peace with the city at the precise moment when, in the middle of a thunderstorm, I gave thanks—never having believed such a thing possible—for still being alive. It was an apocalyptic scene, there under the awning of the Marigny

Theater. The awning served as my umbrella, but it also suddenly became the source of my terror when I realized I'd taken refuge in a place that was no stranger to death.

So clearly do I recall those moments of panic that it feels more appropriate to describe them as if they were happening right now; they are, after all, moments that are always with me.

Before taking cover in the entrance to the Marigny, but seeing there's a downpour on the way, I bound merrily down the Champs-Élysées, convinced that nothing could put a dampener on my good mood. And indeed there's no reason to believe otherwise, because my happiness is born of the knowledge that, at last, in my pocket, I have a French translation of Laurence Sterne's *Tristram Shandy,* a magical book that's proven to be my lucky charm through many a trial. Quite apart from the fact it's exceedingly funny, the book has always given me a strange sort of spiritual strength. And this is why, despite it being a difficult day, with the threat of a violent storm over Paris, I'm skipping along the Champs-Élysées in an exultantly gleeful state of mind.

I stop short on remembering that it's best not to trust happiness, the wisest course of action being to accept it as fleeting and not attempt to hold on to it too tightly. So I rein in my joy and instead try to picture my expression growing steadily more somber as I continue to pick up my pace: a game that I repeat and repeat, until, with the storm now looming overhead, I feel quite serious once more and it finally dawns on me that I need a place to shelter from the rain. I find it beneath the Marigny's splendid awning, but then get the shock of the year when I notice I've positioned myself in the exact spot where, one tragic night, the writer

Ödön von Horváth stood waiting for the film director Robert Siodmak and, finally realizing he'd been stood up, decided to head off, only to be hit by a branch from a chestnut tree that had been struck by lightning, precisely four steps from the awning.

I look at the tree in front of me and feel even more terrified, if such a thing were possible, on finding that it is indeed a chestnut. I reach into my pocket, touch my lucky charm, and try to distract myself with the somewhat unusual story of poor Horváth, who, while walking in the Alps one day, stumbled upon a man who had obviously been dead for many months, no longer a corpse but a skeleton, though with a bag still by his side containing a postcard the dead man had written, which read: "I'm having a wonderful time." Friends asked Horváth what he'd done with the postcard, and he replied: "I found the nearest post office and sent it. What else could I do?"

It wouldn't be so bad, I tell myself, to die struck by lightning in the middle of the Champs-Élysées. It would make for a beautiful ending to my Shandean biography, but then again, I shouldn't rush into anything, my time can't have come just yet. And so I choose to recall the young Ernst Jünger who, in between skirmishes on the battlefield in Bapaume, took great Shandean joy in reading Sterne's masterpiece right there on the front, finding it a source of energy and entertainment in the midst of that disastrous war.

In the young Jünger's case it wasn't the branch of a chestnut tree but a shot that struck him down, though not fatally or even very seriously, since he woke up in a military hospital where he was able to return to his copy of *Tristram Shandy,* which had remained in his coat pocket and, what was more, acted as a handy obstacle to the bullet that sought to kill him. For Jünger, and this is how he recounted it afterward, it was as if everything that happened in between (the gunshot in midcombat, the wound, the hospital, the nurse, his return to reality and also to this weird world) was nothing but a dream or perhaps the contents of Sterne's book itself, a kind of spiritual insert included with the novel.

I'm still stationed under the theater awning, fully aware that venturing out could cost me my life, and giving myself over, now more than ever, to the all-consuming cult of Shandyism, that talisman of mine. There's no question, I tell myself, that the roots of this cult run deep, and that it has a rightful place in this attempt at a "biography of my style" that I think I'm beginning to write.

Lightning strikes.

And it strikes as if to warn me that in no way am I writing a "biography of my style," more like a collection of *untimely prose,* some minor *notes on life and letters* through which I might discover who I really am and who my favorite writer is.

I expect more lightning at any moment. But I'm no longer as afraid, and now turn to face the murderous chestnut tree head-on, while also recalling that Fleur Jaeggy once described how, after writing *Sweet Days of Discipline,* she went back to Appenzell—home province of Robert Walser, the only inhabitant of that literary Cherokee territory par excellence—returning like a murderer to the scene of the crime. The great Fleur went to visit the Swiss girls' boarding school from her novel and discovered it had become a clinic for the blind. Afterward, given that the old boarding school was very close to Herisau, she went to see the mental hospital where Walser had spent twenty-seven years of his life. It was Easter Monday, and at first the only person she saw was a nurse who said she couldn't be much help because she was very busy. Since there was no one else around, Fleur decided to buy some postcards. Immediately, the nurse became more friendly and ended up introducing her to some patients, and Fleur was even able to talk to them. "It was as if I'd taken a journey in Walser's footsteps, looking for the trees that saw him die," Jaeggy remarked after the visit.

I stand perfectly still. The criminal chestnut tree is still there. I'm clearly in a theater and the lightning could be a special effect, although deep down I know that's not true and that when death does come, it won't be in any way that I've previously imagined. Or will it? Of course it will, why shouldn't it? Death doesn't play by the rules.

10

I refuse to give in to the sheer terror. My Shandyism, I tell myself, hasn't accompanied me this far through life only for fear to break me now. Besides, didn't I perfect my courage in Barcelona, in the Friends of Laurence Sterne Society? I smile, mostly at the thought of all the different clubs and societies to which I belong. The Friends of Laurence Sterne Society meets every November 24, when we celebrate the birthday of that great writer, originally from Clonmel, Ireland. James Joyce's followers may have a reputation for being fanatics who breakfast on tea, toast, and pork kidney every June 16, but the friends of Laurence Sterne aren't to be outdone, gathering for dinner every November 24 in a restaurant on the outskirts of Barcelona that's actually called Clonmel and is run by John William Walsh, another native of that Irish town, a fellow who, despite being an insatiable reader, curiously has never been an admirer of the *shandy* world, just as, despite being one of those Irishmen who leave no doubt that they're Irish, he in fact feels more Australian.

Every year at the Clonmel I chuckle to myself when I remember the furious tirades Sterne launches in his book against the more solemn novels of his contemporaries. And every year I'm surprised anew by the book's extremely scant narrative substance; by how the narrator famously isn't even born until very late on. Before that, he's being conceived, which means we can read *Tristram Shandy* as "the gestation of a novel" and be endlessly amused by its constant, glorious digressions and the erudite comments scattered throughout the text.

And above all, I laugh every November 24 at Sterne's great display of Cervantesque irony, remarkable asides to the reader, and use of the stream of consciousness technique that many others would later claim they had invented.

Tristram Shandy is a book whose protagonist doesn't want to be born because he doesn't want to die, just as I don't want to die now on the Champs-Élysées, clinging to my pocket *Tristram* in the vain hope it will provide more effective protection than the awning of the Marigny Theater.

No, I don't want to die and I flick back quickly through my life and see that, ever since it made its first appearance, the *Shandy* comet has always delighted me. I'm fascinated by this novel with its fine thread of a plot and its monologues in which real memories often take the place of imagined events, and where laughter is always just around the corner only to come out as tears instead. Where you discover with a start, on the verge of joyful weeping, that life can be sad. And yes, of course life is sad, just as it can also be *shandy*.

Tristram is not only my amulet but the backbone of everything I've ever written. In that prospective biography of my style, which I've already abandoned, it would no doubt have played a central role. In fact, you can understand almost nothing about me without the incandescent influence of Sterne's book.

Lightning strikes.

11

Yesterday I came across an old message from Tabucchi on my computer, written in an Italian that was heavily littered with Spanish, or vice versa. I read the document with surprise and took it as a sign of something, paying particular attention to a few lines which, due to the manic pace of my life at that time, had slipped my mind completely and which now, removed from their original context, still seem impossible to make sense of, so I've decided to interpret them in a way that suits me.

The message said: "My friend: *che bella sorpresa*. And what a beautiful text. / *Grazie*. And thanks, too, for sharing your latest, *che ci fanno molto piacere*. / You write of a distant past, back in the time of the cetaceans. / An antediluvian age, and yet I lived through it. How strange. / If you come to París, *sarà un piacere ridere di nuovo insieme*. We're here till the end of March. / Warmest wishes, Antonio."

I think, or want to think, that aside from an unlikely yet

always possible allusion to *Moby-Dick,* when Tabucchi mentioned cetaceans he was referring not only to the whales of the Azores but also to *writers from the past,* a special breed, a class of authors who, at the time of his message, had no doubt already begun to go extinct and have since continued disappearing at a considerable pace.

I came across the concept of *writers from the past* in an essay by Fabián Casas, who, referring to Roberto Bolaño, spoke of how much he missed them. People like Julio Cortázar, he said, who weren't merely writers but also "teachers, role models, bright shining lights onto which he and his friends projected themselves."

As I was thinking about this, it dawned on me that I'd always rather lazily assumed there were still some *writers from the past* and other cetaceans around, albeit far fewer than before, when in fact their sort are really more like relics by now, akin to the Paleolithic beings discovered by Herzog, perhaps existing only as traces, marks left behind in caves and scattered here and there among the ruins of modernity.

Marks or traces of the cetacean Lezama Lima in Havana, for example, writing from a tiny abode completely out of keeping with the magnitude of his great Whale-Work. And traces, too, of Roberto Bolaño himself, laughing away in his cave in Blanes and flaunting his magnificent refusal to conform to the work of those contemporaries whose writing he didn't like, which was most of them, although his opinions were liable to change. Understandable, really, given that he liked to be arbitrary and make lists and not take literature too seriously, which, in my opinion, has always been the best way of taking it in any way seriously.

"The writer's trade is a pretty miserable one, but it's also full of fools who don't realize how immensely fragile, how ephemeral it is," Bolaño once said on Chilean television. I don't know if he'd agree—probably not, because he liked to be contrary—but personally, whenever someone spoke to me about "a true writer," or "a *writer from the past,*" or any writer you could actually call a writer, and who wasn't just another impostor, I always, always pictured him—and still do—dressed head to toe in black and looking very French (even if he didn't have a French bone in his body), gazing out at the Mediterranean. And I imagined this writer as a poet as well, somewhere far beyond the poetry of Chile or France.

"A poet," Bolaño also said, "can endure anything. Which amounts to saying that a human being can endure anything." But Bolaño wasn't satisfied with the second statement, because he believed there was little a man could endure, whereas a poet could withstand anything.

Really? I believe, or want to believe, that the poetry world is also full of fools. According to W. H. Auden, one such fool was Alfred Tennyson, who went around in his youth looking like a gypsy and later on like a dirty old monk. For Auden, Tennyson was the English poet with the finest ear, though probably also the biggest fool of them all.

12

Mallarmé was no fool, he had a very fine ear, and he really could endure anything, with his timeless air of a reclusive poet inside his house on the Rue de Rome. It was a closed-off, homely place, "with a musty smell of pipe tobacco, old silks and ancient scrolls," which is how I'd imagined his study in my second book, a novella that, over time, I got into the habit of describing to interested parties as "capable of killing anyone who read it." In fact, that claim masked the immense panic I felt at the thought of having readers. And no doubt that's why I built a villainous storytelling machine that murdered anyone who laid eyes on those lethal pages and discovered how inexpert a writer I was, though perhaps not so inept when it came to inflicting death by means of my work . . . .

Was Mallarmé's musty smell uniquely French? In the same way that the equally musty Miles Davis might have been when I saw him play in around 1965 at the Palau de la Música Catalana in Barcelona. The trumpeter performed with his back to the public, competing against the shouting and heckling coming from the then terribly bigoted jazz enthusiasts in that Francoist city, who were all convinced that "the black man" kept his back to them as a gesture of contempt.

I was fascinated by this idea of turning one's back on the audience and used it to justify why, in my second book, I turned my back on everyone and, as if that weren't enough, set out to kill the reader. When I reflect on the period in which I wrote it, I also remember "the kitchen of the text," namely everything that's not in the book itself but behind it, and then I clearly recall that in my head the whole novel took place among "old silks and ancient scrolls"; that is, it was set in my imagined idea of Mallarmé's study, at 89 Rue de Rome, Paris.

And I remember, too, that I used to entertain myself by having Miles Davis visit Mallarmé, always with the same purpose: to encourage him to finish the poem he was working on, like any French writer worth his salt. On one of his visits, it seems Miles Davis asked Mallarmé how he saw his oeuvre within the history of literature. And Mallarmé, keeping in mind that Miles Davis hadn't even been born yet, told him there would come a time when literature would be recognized as an end in itself, that is, without God or any external justification or supporting ideology. A discipline in its own right.

When that day comes, Mallarmé told Davis, you'll be long dead, and as for me, the less said the better. Miles Davis smiled, set down his trumpet on a blue silk armchair, and after thinking for a long time (he didn't want to come across as stupid) said:

"Could it be that you write about the very thing that hinders your writing? And could it be that I play jazz because it speaks to what hinders my playing?"

Unbeknown to him, with that question Davis anticipated the words of Samuel Beckett many years later: "That which hinders painting is itself painted."

"Jazz?" Mallarmé asked.

The question was so difficult that the answer never came, and Mallarmé realized that even though he was talking to someone, deep down he was alone.

13

I can hardly contain my excitement as I prepare to say this: the writers I like the most are the very model of the coldest, most rapierlike intelligence, the ones who push to the limit what someone once called the "frightful discipline of the spirit." And that's it; I could finish there. But I think it's worth adding that perhaps the quality I most admire in "French writers" is their absolute autonomy. Because the truly extraordinary thing about literature is that it's a space of such immense freedom that it allows for all kinds of contradictions. For instance, within a single paragraph you can both believe and not believe in Madeleine Moore. Liz Themerson's stories also come to mind, in which the epiphany of faith and the epiphany of the most radical Nothingness go hand in hand and it's impossible to tell if Themerson is a believer, a non-believer, or just unfailingly ambiguous.

"French writers" include, to give some examples, Clarice Lispector, Julien Gracq, Ida Vitale, Felisberto Hernández, Felipe Polleri, Harry Mathews, Madeleine Moore, and the Comte de Lautréamont.

Not forgetting Jean-Yves Jouannais, who, in his particular case, as in that of Moore and Gracq, is also French by birth and thus doubly French, if you like, though I'm not sure you can be doubly French because the numbers don't add up: either you're a real writer (in which case you're French, even if you're actually Norwegian), or you're not: a good example being God, who, when he writes, is anything but French.

14

Jouannais is a man in pursuit of an obsession: chronicling all of the wars throughout history. His lectures, or performances, at the Beaubourg in Paris—one a month for more than a decade, as part of his *Encyclopedia of Wars* cycle—have always been dramatic events: a kind of endless mise-en-scène in which, session after session, Jouannais—always wearing his grandfather's military ID bracelet and the pocket watch that belonged to his great-grandfather, an artilleryman killed in the Battle of the Somme—dramatizes the writing process of his vast, boundless *Encyclopedia.*

This *Encyclopedia,* as you can imagine, spans from the *Iliad* to the present day, and because of its inexhaustible nature, the project looks set to go on indefinitely, which perhaps affords Jouannais some peace of mind when it comes to the matter of the published book, because nothing calms you down like knowing you don't have to say everything when the Everything you've chosen as your focus is quite clearly immeasurable. At heart, Jouannais is a poet, working on the endless draft of a novel he will never have to publish, there being neither the time nor the materials in the world to print it, and for which, as a result, he will never have to decide on a definitive form.

Sometimes I think it's not a bad idea to write a book we know won't be finished even by the end of our life. It reminds me of Macedonio Fernández, Borges's mentor, who began writing *The Museum of Eterna's Novel* in 1925 and carried on for twenty-seven years until death interrupted his work, thereby guaranteeing that *The Museum of Eterna's Novel* remained truly eternal—eternally unfinished. In fact, that *Novel* is more of an "antinovel," a nonlinear narrative including all kinds of reflections, discussions, and games, not to mention fifty prologues before the supposed main story starts. When it was published in Argentina in 1965, thirteen years after Macedonio's death, it quickly became clear that, rather like one of those decapitated soldiers who go stumbling on across the battlefield without a head, *The Museum of*

Eterna's Novel was one of those books that has a *life of its own.* In other words, it goes on novelizing itself.

Jouannais clearly knows a thing or two about books with a life of their own. I think it's fair to say we've been friends for years, despite never having laid eyes on each other—or only once, across a room at the Beaubourg, when neither of us made any attempt to go over and say hello. And I've always believed there was something deliberate, on both our parts, about this "friendly" nonencounter.

Our never having greeted each other, our mutual shying away from an actual meeting, might be because our relationship was founded on an intense epistolary correspondence, which we later refused to betray by switching to email or to vulgar, effusive hugs in public. Our friendship, therefore, pays tribute to the almost entirely defunct world of written correspondence, to the golden age, to the world of letters, nowadays mercilessly diminished and in complete, tragic decline.

All this somehow reminds me that my great friendship with Madeleine Moore has carried on over the years in large part because she doesn't understand much Spanish and my French has always been less than perfect. I remember the day Madeleine told her friend Dominique González-Foerster: "If he and I had understood everything we were saying to each other, I'm sure our friendship would be less intense by now."

Jouannais, a *writer from the past,* embodies one version of narrative trend number three, reserved for those who don't say everything. And in fact, even if he wanted to say everything—in his case, to tell the story of every war that's ever been—he would of course be held back by internal factors, by obstacles inherent to his own literary project. In a way, he reminds us of Miles Davis's question to Mallarmé: "Could it be that you write about the very thing that hinders your writing?"

15

In this, the age of emails, I receive a long, handwritten letter from Enzo Cuadrelli, "Modugno" to some, because of his—to my mind vague—resemblance to the singer. A writer from my generation, a professor and novelist, originally from La Plata in Argentina but for the last five years based in New York, and before that in Boston, where he'd also been a professor, at Boston University. A friend ever since our long-ago first meeting in Matanchén Bay. More friend than foe, I think, though I've never been entirely sure.

In his letter, he writes that Buenos Aires has just seen the biggest tornadoes in its history, leaving seventeen dead, many more injured, and one hundred thousand trees felled. But he doesn't live in Buenos Aires, he reminds me, and then concludes his brief opening remarks: "Needless to say, I'm glad I live in New York, although a tornado could happen here at any time." In the second, longer part of the letter, he tells me he's finishing a book about the figure of "that shady man who refuses point blank to do anything," namely Bartleby the office clerk, and then adds that he's collected a great deal of biographical data on the character who, after all, despite being an invention of Herman Melville, has a biography like everyone else. "It's a book," Cuadrelli concludes, "that purposely brushes aside the ever more insufferable Melvillian cliché of 'I would prefer not to,' which, might I add, you used so very liberally in *Virtuosos of Suspense*."

Cuadrelli can't have known the joy I'd feel at these words, let alone at his marvelous decision to crush, once and for all, that tired old "I would prefer not to," for which I'd developed a genuine loathing.

Oh, I'd been waiting so long for someone to release me from that excruciating phrase, that ghastly cliché that's haunted me ever since I published *Virtuosos of Suspense,* in which, some twenty years ago, I investigated cases of writers affected by that syndrome "of the No" I called "Rimbaud syndrome"! Over time that book became a nightmare, one I've learned to live with in recent years, a nightmare buried under my skin like the apple Gregor Samsa's father threw at him, which lodged itself in Gregor's flesh and eventually rotted.

Back when I wrote *Virtuosos of Suspense* I'd been interested in exploring the world of those writers who, prolific or not, allowed themselves to be carried away by the negative drive or the allure of Nothingness, and stopped writing altogether. But the problem with this book haunting me, a problem I've been sensing on the horizon for some time, is that any day now I might very well turn into a victim of my own syndrome.

If that were to happen—and sometimes I can see it coming—I'd accept it as a new experience, and at the same time as a fate that I had after all, I'd think, predicted. But I'd still be cross with myself, because I couldn't say I hadn't been amply warned by Antonio Tabucchi, among others, that something like this might happen. One evening at Siete Puertas, a restaurant in Barcelona, Tabucchi told me that so much talk of Rimbaud might lead to writer's block. This could hardly be news, he added, especially considering that the whole legend around that poet in Western culture was based on a *small, trivial inaccuracy,* since Rimbaud didn't abandon literature because he felt he had nothing more to say but simply out of choice.

"As soon as you publish your Bartleby biography, which will expose the *I would prefer* cliché for what it is," I wrote in my reply to Cuadrelli, "it will have my full and wholehearted support. It couldn't have come at a better time for me, and I couldn't be more in favor of putting an end to the hackneyed rattling out of the scrivener's catchphrase."

In the second part of my letter I reminded him what his fellow Argentinean Bioy Casares once said about the happy fate enjoyed by some books and how much this success sometimes irked their authors, which is exactly what's been happening to me for years now, like a kind of curse, with *Virtuosos of Suspense,* a novel I wrote without a care in the world and that has haunted me ever since in a most worrying way, as if it were the only book I'd ever written: "There are works that have a pathetically unhappy fate. What a man wrote in his most lucid fervor simply withers, burned away by a secret desire to die, and what he wrote just for fun, or to meet an obligation, endures, as if its carefree creation bestowed upon it the kiss of immortality."

16

Carefree Creation is a good title, isn't it? Tabucchi died before I could ask him this question, and many others besides.

I admired his imagination as well as his ability to delve into reality and end up in a parallel, deeper version of it; the reality that sometimes accompanies the one we can see. I remember he was fond of Drummond de Andrade, the Brazilian poet who envisioned the mystery of the great beyond as no more than an old frozen palace. I think about this as I knock on the gates of lost time and find that no one answers. I knock again, and again the feeling comes that my knocking is in vain.

The house of lost time is covered in ivy on one side and ashes on the other. A deserted house, and yet here I am knocking and crying out from the pain of crying out and not being heard. Nothing clearer than the fact that lost time doesn't exist; only the empty, sealed house. And the old frozen palace.

Tabucchi's death is haunting me, to the point that I'm now remembering that trip to Corvo, the most remote island of the Azores. It can be reached only by rowboat or launch. I'll never forget the day we both landed there and saw a man who owned a windmill for crushing grain and who couldn't believe there were still people who bothered to visit Corvo, the least inhabited of all the Azores.

"Gentlemen, may I ask what brings you here?"

"One goes to Corvo for going's sake," Tabucchi replied.

17

Some time after that foray onto Corvo, I'm sitting in the last seat of the last carriage of the TGV from Bordeaux to Lyon. It's winter in France and I'm due to give a lecture as part of a series called "The Coming of Winter." It's a thorny topic. Winter comes every year, is all I can think of to say. Or: In Barcelona the winters are mild. But the choice of topic is not all that surprising. By now I'm quite used to lecture series that tackle unconventional themes. Indeed, I have a good deal of experience of being invited to conferences on topics all equally unusual and finding without fail that the insatiable creative force behind these events is one Yvette Sánchez, a professor at the University of St. Gallen.

Conferences on failure, on the world of wayward bonsai trees, on fatal showers in cinema, on the enigmatic joy of the bears in Bern . . . . Given these past topics, the somewhat gratuitous-sounding theme of the Lyon gathering, "The Coming of Winter," doesn't particularly faze me. If you think about it, it's a broad, inexhaustible matter, and full of possibilities. Admittedly, it's also one I'm embarrassed to address in public. And what's more, I'm nervous, because I haven't prepared anything. Still, I'll give it a shot. But how mortifying if I go blank and end up desperately hoping that the coming of winter will coincide with the coming of some inspiration.

I'm thinking about all this on the TGV as I gaze out of the window. I've yet to take a single train journey where the window doesn't remind me, however briefly, of the old story about W. H. Auden, who was crossing the Alps by train with some friends and sat engrossed in his book while his companions cooed ecstatically over the majestic landscape; in the space of a few seconds, he glanced up from his book and out of the carriage window, before returning to his reading with the words: "One look is enough."

Every train window reminds me, not of the coming of

winter, but of Auden's attitude and what he said, which in turn brings to mind Don Quixote and how he would catch one glimpse of reality and let his imagination do the rest.

I look through the glass and see, in the distance, smoke rising from the chimneys of some houses near Limoges. That's also the coming of winter, I say to myself. And I remember, almost miraculously, two lines by Julien Gracq in which he talks about that one cold draft that we feel out of nowhere when we still think it's fall: winter making its presence felt, turning up in the form of a "chill that flows close to the ground and, having snuck in, shows no intention of leaving."

I was very struck when I read those lines by the great Gracq, which seemed to be saying: Every second is full of signs for us, but almost all of them go unnoticed. And I remember how my strong reaction soon gave way to the fascination I still feel for that image of cold and death flowing along close to the ground. So much so that I'm thinking about it right now and wondering if I could build an entire lecture around it. The lecture, I tell myself, should last one minute, or the few seconds it took Auden to look up from his book and out of the train window.

In the buffet car I feel scared at the very thought of how ashamed I'll be if my lecture turns out to be a disaster. I'm scared of going blank, as I do at the most terrifying moments in my dreams. But then I remember someone saying that shame is a great thing because it sharpens your wits. And surely even that falls short, as Elizabeth Hardwick observed in *Sleepless Nights,* recalling a trip she made years ago on a Canadian train from Montreal to Kingston, when she realized that, out of shame, before setting off, she'd taken inordinate care over her appearance: clothes, shoes, rings, watches, accents, teeth, mannerisms—anything that might reflect parts of her personality.

By the time I leave the buffet car, I'm getting an idea of the scene my lecture will focus on. It will of course be related to the coming of winter, and it will also feature a never-before-seen Baudelaire, a Baudelaire in Paris listening to the constant sound of logs being dropped onto the city's cobbled courtyards. Logs being unloaded from carts, outside house after house, as the cold sets in. The logs fall to the ground and Baudelaire is hiding nearby, listening keenly to the monotonous sounds as they land. Not much else will happen in this scene with the crouching poet, except that Baudelaire will listen to everything, study it, analyze it, sensing with horror that the modern age will play out to the thudding of logs against cobblestones.

He didn't like modern life, but at the same time it fascinated him. He was very ambiguous, Antoine Compagnon tells us in *Irreducible Baudelaire,* because his antimodernity actually represented an authentic modernity, which resisted modern life despite being irremissibly committed to it. Doesn't all this remind us that "to be truly contemporary one must be *untimely*"? And isn't that what Nietzsche was saying in Turin when he cried that "to be truly contemporary" we must be slightly old-fashioned, maintaining a critical distance that allows us to sketch out a political divergence from the present?

And amid all that spying on logs landing in cobbled courtyards, amid all Baudelaire's investigations, that coarse, repetitive music of the moment will eventually merge, like a kindred spirit, with the poet's habit, his far from noble—and indeed rather shadowy, sordid, and endlessly repeated—practice of abusing his friends' kindness. Someone once described it as psychotic, pointing to how the poet was always, so to speak, "on his last logs." "As I write this, I'm burning my last two logs" was a common refrain in his letters. It's true he was penniless, but he had only himself to blame. He had shunned work all his life and was paying the price. In short, I think I've got the start of my lecture: "Ladies and gentlemen, I always call the coming of winter 'Baudelaire.'"

18

After my experiences on Calle del Hambre, which were really an extension of the years I spent wrestling with the almost total void, I reappeared in Paris in the late eighties, full of plans but with no real intention of carrying any of them out. By then I had three published books to my name, all of them rather irregular, and the distinct impression—or indeed the certainty—that I'd made my entrance into the literary world, which in practice simply meant that there'd now be some people passing judgment on my work without having read it first.

During my second spell in Paris, the only one of my old *copains* I looked up was Madeleine Moore, since I had her address and we'd carried on a lively written correspondence. In those days, she was making her name as a performance artist, and also as a discerning art critic. We agreed to meet at La Closerie des Lilas, which Madeleine called "the house of the devil Vauvert," because apparently that famous ghost, so integral to all of Paris's legends, had lived for a time in the crumbling basements of the mansion that existed there before La Closerie.

Vauvert was an old Parisian who used to pop up without fail in the most varied neighborhoods of the city, and indeed across the centuries. He was by now about six hundred years old, and much-loved among the locals. In fact, people went as far as to say he was the incarnation of the raging Parisian masses. The rumor that he might have been haunting La Closerie was such common knowledge that, when the establishment first opened, Hemingway took the bait: he would go there to write in the mornings, before the other customers were let in, and sit at a bright table in the window reserved just for him. Everything suggests that Hemingway was inspired, however unwittingly, by the atmosphere Vauvert left in his wake whenever he drifted by.

I was taken aback when I saw Moore walk through La Closerie's revolving door. She looked luminous, with a startling new confidence. The young woman I'd met all those years ago, so intelligent yet so fragile, struggling with all sorts of problems, had found a way of escaping the traps life had set for her in her early years. It was inspiring to re-encounter Moore, to see how she'd managed to turn things around and replace the daily dealing of cocaine wraps with other, less risky activities.

I've never forgotten how, on that second trip of mine to Paris, Moore confessed that she'd like to be a writer one day—of a single book, she stated, which is indeed what came to pass: there hasn't been another, and nor will there be—and then explained to me at great length that we were heading toward a future that we'd be forced to share with all kinds of writers seduced by the digital world and the possible ways technology might change how we read. And I'm always amazed to recall just how right she was.

Now listen, Moore had said, there's no point fighting the digital idiots, because there are idiots in every field. We have to listen to what the idiots say, understand them, and then create a world for ourselves where they can't get in.

Over time, I think, both she and I have created that world for ourselves, though I to a lesser degree. What she said that day made a lot of sense, because it's since become clear that Moore's only book does something truly original, in that it situates itself outside of the problematic critical currents of the last half century. In fact, Moore writes as if untouched by debates around first-person narration, autofiction (a genre that doesn't actually exist, because anything you write always comes from yourself and is therefore autofictional; even the Bible is autofiction, because it begins with someone creating something), self-representation, nonfiction (which doesn't exist either, because any written version of a true story is always a kind of fiction—the moment the world is arranged into words, it is fundamentally altered).

19

Moore's thoughts on digital idiots might have been the only unforgettable thing about that reunion had it not been for what happened when we asked for the check, which we thought at first was taking a long time to arrive but then began to suspect would never come at all. We must have asked those renowned waiters for it five times, but they seemed to be following instructions from *Maître* Vauvert. We even tried asking God and Kafka's uncle, but there was no getting through to them; they remained unmoved by our polite request to pay. And it was all so irritating, and at the same time so devilishly funny, that we felt the situation required us to take some sort of action, or even to retaliate. So we did. Since Moore had her Citroën DS parked right opposite La Closerie, she suggested we slip out without paying, and when the moment arose, without a second thought, we made our way to the revolving door—in which, for one fraught moment, we almost got stuck—and onto the Boulevard du Montparnasse, where we scrambled into her car and made our gleeful getaway, jubilant at having successfully pulled off what, in the moment, felt really quite transgressive, since there was something rather invincible about La Closerie.

I would tell the story of that hasty getaway years later, at the Hôtel Le Littré, in an interview for *Libération,* and the journalist must have spread it around in the following months because one day a television writer short on ideas got in touch and asked to take me back to that revolving door and, while the waiters made a show of languid surveillance, had me restage the great escape.

I remember how, during my reenactment, I thought I'd pretend to be trapped in the revolving door for a few seconds, pulling it off so realistically that for a moment I was afraid the waiters would take the opportunity to present me with the original check and demand that I pay up there and then, with the corresponding colossal accumulated interest.

And I also remember that, just in case that happened, I was primed with the response that Josep Pla, much to the embarrassment of his fellow diners—journalists, writers, and other inquisitive types who would travel up from Barcelona to see him and trust that the *maestro* would pick up the tab—used to give at what was then the Motel Ampurdán in Figueres when presented with the lunch check:

"No tenim diners. Som escriptors." (We don't have any money. We're writers.)

20

Some time after that foray onto Corvo, I find myself in Saint-Germain, a few yards from the green bench I still consider to be mine, if only because I once had a long conversation with Tabucchi there about the suicide in the Azores of the great poet of those islands, Antero de Quental.

At noon I made my way to the terrace of Les Deux Magots, and now here I am, waiting for Moore, who, after a break in her long trajectory as a creator of all kinds of "artistic actions," has just published *La concession française,* which, just as she's always promised, will be the first and only book she ever writes. I've come to this terrace because she asked me to join her for an interview she has scheduled with *Chic to Cheek,* during which I fully intend to keep my bitterness about her book title—I wish I'd thought of it myself—under wraps.

Seeing myself sitting so placidly on this terrace, I don't seem like a potential catalyst of chaos, and yet inside I'm extremely worked up. I can't stop thinking about Moore and her book, which, quite aside from the brilliant title, stands out for its author's remarkably ruthless refusals to conform; that is, for the originality and good taste she displays in her rejection of the latest trends in contemporary literature.

And while I'm mulling this over and hoping she gets here soon, I can't stop imagining what I would ask her if I were the interviewer, as long as I didn't work for a magazine like *Chic to Cheek,* whose interviewers never fail to dream up the most inane—when not downright stupid—questions.

While I wait for Moore, I tell myself she'll no doubt turn up with René, her long-term boyfriend, a young filmmaker with a passion for sixties cinema. Godard's *Weekend,* for example, which was indirectly inspired by Cortázar's story "The Southern Thruway," which I believe was in turn inspired by Buñuel's movie *The Exterminating Angel.*

I found *La concession française* so thrilling because of the extreme demands it makes on its readers. And I feel a deep admiration for Moore and her ways; she seems to go from strength to strength. Last week someone described her quite perceptively as an artist who explores a sort of *expanded literature,* that is, who enters and operates within other artforms, including the ambiguous art of "appearances" and "disappearances." As an artist, Moore metabolizes references of all kinds—literary and cinematic, architectural and musical, scientific and pop—and creates "rooms," "interiors," "gardens," and "planets" like no one else. Among her many projects in the pipeline is "Alienarium 5," which will ask what would happen if aliens were to fall in love with us— what would change, and how and why.

I'm waiting for her, but also for the journalist, who's late. Or am I early? I didn't sleep a wink last night and I keep nearly nodding off in my Deux Magots chair, a situation at once unsettling and thoroughly liberating.

As if in a nod to the book's title, in *La concession française* Moore doesn't make the slightest concession to lazy readers.

And she often links the text to her usual "artistic actions," which in recent times have focused on exploring the tangled mess of identity that ensnares each and every one of us.

Would it be such a drama to lose our identity? The question runs through the entire book, from start to finish. The daughter of a British soldier—who committed suicide when she was five years old—and a mother from Marseille who inherited a large fortune of apparently dubious origins, Moore has divided her life between Paris and Rio de Janeiro, with one long and mysterious period in Shanghai, where I attempted to visit her, even making it as far as the front of the house by the sea where she lived, in the strictest anonymity, but never actually managing to see her, thus discovering that "strictest anonymity," in this case actually meant total anonymity. That unusual experience—traveling all that way to see someone who says they're waiting for you by the East China Sea and then not so much as chancing upon that person—inspired me to write a book I called *The Wrong Move,* like the Wim Wenders movie, which I was a big fan of at the time.

I sit and I wait. Not wanting to appear idle, and yet on the verge of a truly ridiculous accidental catnap in front of all the other people on the terrace, who I know love to keep a close critical eye on what's going on around them, I leaf through *La concession française,* although all I'm really doing is reading and rereading the brilliantly apt quote from Flaubert that opens the book: "Art is a luxury; it requires a clean, steady hand. First we make a small concession, which turns into two, then twenty."

There's nothing strange, I tell myself, about Moore having written such a perfect book, but I say it without moving past that page, because I've already read the whole thing twice, and right now my most pressing concern is to make a good impression on the distinguished and not-so-distinguished patrons of Les Deux Magots, among whom I think I spot Jean-Pierre Léaud. Yes, it's him. But when I meet his eye, he goes from being deadly serious to laughing uproariously to himself.

I'm waiting for Moore, and in my mind now I'm just kicking stones, like back in my teenage days, when nothing ever happened to me and I lived in the deepest of voids.

I'm waiting for her and recalling how she sometimes says she's waiting for the One Great Reader, because she demands that her readers engage on a deeply personal level with what she writes. It's as if she wanted to address individual intellects and conquer them one by one, intellects with nothing in common but the wish to escape unanimity. "She seems to write purely for those beings who seek, for themselves alone, a detailed description of their private abysses," said Tabucchi, who was amazed by what he read of *La concession française,* part of the first draft, back when he was in Paris and renting a small apartment on Rue de l'Université.

Speaking of Tabucchi, I'm inclined to think that, as with the island of Corvo, we go to Moore's unique world *for going's sake* and always in the knowledge that we'll see something new. Moore should be proud of the extraordinary determination with which she rejects all the dozens of different literary avenues that make up *La concession française.* Indeed, it's almost astonishing how many paths she spurned before coming up with that voice, so distinct and so hard not to hear in her only book.

21

Meanwhile, the interviewer has just arrived. I recognize him straight away because he reminds me of the late, great Swiss actor Michel Simon. His resemblance to that now somewhat forgotten star—who shone especially brightly in the legendary Jean Vigo movie *The Passing Barge*—is disconcerting, and this perhaps explains why, rather intimidated, I can't think of anything to say aside from inviting him to take a seat at what I assure him will become, in a matter of minutes, the table of "Madame Madeleine Moore."

At which point Moore arrives, without René. Bleary-eyed, as if she were still carrying around the hazy dreams of the night before. I make the introductions. Then comes the first question from the fake Simon, followed by many more, until I grow tired of saying nothing and interrupt the interviewer to ask Moore a question of my own, one to which she reels off a robotic response while at the same time appearing thoroughly grateful for the opportunity to do so:

"A strong tendency to seek extreme perfection in one's work. Does that make sense?"

That's just it, I think. Both she and I have always greatly valued how, for some of us writers, dedication to our work is our only moral stance.

Moore's swift response must have made it look as if we'd rehearsed the scene. And now, after hearing it, the man from *Chic to Cheek* seems to have shifted the focus of his questions and even, to my surprise, considerably raised the tone.

"When it comes to putting pen to paper, what's most tempting for a woman writer nowadays?"

Where have I heard that question before? Never mind, it's almost identical to mine, only worded differently, and what matters now is that it's far superior to the ones this Simon lookalike has been asking up until this point. Moore's answer, however, only ends up sowing confusion, as she pretends to be offended by his interest—when in fact nobody has asked her about any such thing—in the days she spent off the radar in China.

"If it's not in *La concession française,* do you really expect me to reveal to you now what I did on the outskirts of Shanghai during my most secret days?"

I laugh silently at the interviewer's look of utter bewilderment.

And it's true. In the book, Moore's only reference to Shanghai comes when she mentions the two years she spent working at the big hotel known at the time as the Cathay, which were followed by another two in a "contemporary art" gallery a stone's throw from Yu Garden, after which, quite inexplicably, she disappeared off to a house by the sea, until she was eventually sighted again strolling along the legendary Bund one winter's day and telling everyone about the thing she'd been so sorry to leave behind: her old black stove, which was always burning, like a symbol of eternal fire, in a house on the central coast of China.

22

"Did you know we've been looking for Goya's head for two centuries now?" I hear Moore being asked.

I can't believe my ears. Why is the interviewer talking

about a head? And Goya's head, at that! Just then, I have a sudden sense that something's not quite right with my own head, at which point I wake with a start from the momentary nap I'd let myself sink into right there in the middle of Les Deux Magots and confirm that the interviewer has indeed just asked that question about Goya. But I must have missed something. Perhaps my unintentional snooze lasted longer than I thought. I would never have imagined that, however lost I became in the obscure mists of a Paris café dream, I'd be able to form so many opinions about *La concession française*. Most of all I worry I've been talking in my sleep, which would explain the disgruntled look on Moore's face. I hope she hasn't found out that my dream-self thought her blunt, stripped-down prose sometimes revealed a certain lack of substance, and at other times, total vacuity.

The main problem is that, now I'm awake, I still feel critical of the book, even mercilessly so, and I hardly recognize myself as I conspire, alone and in silence, against my genius friend, which amounts to conspiring against myself, indeed to a kind of self-harm, and perhaps that's why I now make out like I'm checking thoroughly to see if my head is in my hands or whether it's still attached, and end up wondering if that unknown thing inside me is what's helping me begin to understand myself at last.

As if the action weren't unfolding decisively enough, the interviewer can't think of anything better than to ask Moore what writing ultimately means to her. She fires back a devastating response, probably rehearsed in advance at home:

"Writing, as Dr. Johnson said, is expressing oneself through letters, it's recording, printing, getting the words down, acting like an author, talking through books, laughing at the Belgian flies, banishing the Earth from the solar system, extracting something from nothing, it's speaking without being interrupted . . . ."

On seeing her deviate so far from Dr. Johnson's English dictionary, I interrupt her Kalashnikov-style rapid-fire response to announce that I don't believe in inner worlds. At this, the Earth seems to stop turning, as if it really had left the solar system. Terrifying. When it starts up again, I explain to Moore that I only said I didn't believe in inner worlds as a way of stopping her in her tracks and preventing the interview from going on much longer.

Moore looks so horrified that all of a sudden I want nothing more than to disappear from there as quickly as possible. In fact, I even try to do just that by retreating—oh, the irony—into my own inner world, into the memory of a trip I took years ago to the asylum in Herisau, in the Swiss canton of Appenzell, when I happened to see a young and spectacularly tall clergyman—about six foot five—peering out from the doorway of a church in Straubenzell.

"Oh, no! The clergy are coming for us," said Yvette Sánchez, my good friend from St. Gallen, the organizer of all those unusual conferences, and the reason for that foray into a very special part of Switzerland, the spiritual as well as geographical terrain of Robert Walser. With us, I clearly recall, was her Austrian friend Beatrix, who smiled at that comment about our priestly pursuers, perhaps because she'd heard all about the horrendous dinner the night before and my pointless, absurd argument with a venerated Swiss priest and friend of Yvette's. At the same time, I remembered a story about Robert Walser, who once, while walking with his friend Carl Seelig, saw a young friar gazing out of a monastery window and remarked: "He's nostalgic for the outside world, just as we yearn for the inner one."

I'm still immersed in my inner world and the memory of that trip to Herisau when Beatrix's car rounds a bend in the road and I, momentarily losing my way, find myself back once again in Les Deux Magots, where Moore remains stony-faced and I've been searching in vain for a safe mental space in which to hide away for a few minutes, only to find that St. Gallen wasn't it and no others seemed to be available, meaning that in the end I was forced to give up and leave myself emotionally exposed.

"Where would you like to be right now?" the interviewer asks.

And Moore replies, increasingly animated:

"I'd like there to be stable, unmoving, intangible places, places that are references, starting points, moral principles. And I'd like for you to take a flying leap."

The journalist goes deadly silent, while Moore, surely trying to make it up to me, gives me a warm look and, referring to the journalist, says:

"What can I say? He's clearly not Wittgenstein."

The shot-down interviewer won't recover from this blow. Soon afterward, we'll watch him leave, head bowed and without saying goodbye, in the direction of Odeón. And we'll notice how, the farther away he gets, the more his shadow veers from one side of the boulevard to the other.

23

I ask myself whether *La concession française* could be considered a natural heir to Valéry's proposals for the contemporary novel. And the quickest and most honest answer is that no, it couldn't. As I see it, a more fitting successor to those Valerian proposals—which are, in fact, linked to the structure of René Descartes's *Discourse on Method*—would be, for example, what we might call "the partial novel of a brain" that Rodrigo Fresán created in *The Invented Part,* the first volume of what seems set to become a trilogy about the cogs and wheels that make the mind of a contemporary writer tick.

There are other books along this, shall we say, cerebral line, but the example of *The Invented Part* is enough to give an idea of the kind of writing I'm talking about, and which, coincidentally or not, is connected to *Monsieur Teste,* where Valéry writes in his author´s preface to the second edition: "In this strange head, where philosophy has little weight, where language is always in question, there is scarcely any thought free of the sense that it is provisional."

Mr. Teste spends his brief, intense life supervising the mechanism by which the links between the known and the unknown are established and organized. Rodrigo Fresán oversees the same mechanism, albeit honing in on the type of literary creation that invents the unknown every morning. Fresán is also connected to the great stylist John Banville. Both writers are more committed to language and its rhythms than to plot, characters, or narrative pace.

All the fundamental books in my reading life take place inside a head, and that's what I've worked to bring about myself, as a writer, says Fresán, who is predominantly interested in telling the story of style, or of the search for style, a process that turns the how into the what. After all, Fresán also believes that when it comes to the most groundbreaking books—be it *Ulysses, Tristram Shandy, Don Quixote,* or *Moby-Dick*—the plot can be summed up in roughly three sentences.

Sometimes I think *The Invented Part* could easily have taken its title from a characteristically Valerian line, a key phrase from 1902, in his *Cahiers:*

"Other people make books. I am making my mind."

So this is the way that Valéry's least spurious line of succession seems to run, down a path perhaps opened up in one of his many letters to André Gide, a fellow writer of his generation. Gide and Valéry exchanged some six hundred letters, a bafflingly high number considering that the two men couldn't have been more different. For one thing, Gide was inspired and even excited by reading other people, while Valéry was either nonplussed or positively irritated by what others wrote, and if he did admit to reading it, it was only to confirm his own prejudices. In his letters to Gide, Valéry repeatedly expressed his misgivings about novelists, be they expert storytellers or the kind who deliberately said nothing or who leave a perfidious or sometimes very simple loose thread in their stories.

Writers! How could Valéry appreciate them when he felt they injected endless discomfort into his veins, to the point that every day he felt more disgusted by *the activity of story-telling?* For the most part, Valéry couldn't stand novels, and in a passage that did the rounds in France at the time, he wrote that he *was not made for them,* because "their great scenes, tirades, passions, and tragic moments, far from enthusing me, reach me like miserable outbursts, rudimentary states in which all foolishness is let loose, in which a being is simplified to the point of absurdity."

24

"Paris," I say out of nowhere, believing the word alone to be capable of expressing an entire state of mind. But does saying "Paris" say everything? Maybe I'm wrong to think so, or maybe not, because for me Paris is Beckett when he began to say everything and committed to carrying on endlessly down the path of *Finnegans Wake,* though without moving, like the two characters in *Waiting for Godot:*

> "VLADIMIR: Well? Shall we go?
> ESTRAGON: Yes, let's go.
> They do not move."

"Paris," I say to myself. "A stable, unmoving, intangible place."

Strangest of all is what happens later, when I repeat to a horrified Moore what had so enraged her before: I tell her I don't believe in inner worlds at all, and I think I say it as an act of pure self-harm; I can't find any other explanation.

I don't move. I'm ready to face the consequences.

As I await the coming storm, I realize I've let myself be carried away by my inner devil Vauvert and by the desire to undermine the calm stability of the moment. And I've managed it. The look on Moore's face tells me she's now fully aware that I found more flaws in her book than she expected.

And perhaps for that reason, because she's now fully

noted that, half secretly, but also half giving myself away, I disagree with the odd passage in *La concession française,* Moore swells with indignation. Beyond anything I could have foreseen, which leads me to think that my best friend— the one I've always considered "my genius friend"—might well get up and walk out.

And yet that won't happen. I realize this shortly afterward when I see that she's staying put, wonderfully stable, unmoving, intangible, like Paris, allowing me to remember the day I discovered I could indulge in secret intellectual passions, like the one that grows within me as I write this text, involving Paul Valéry's writing, as well as his ungodly writing schedule, always subject to a preternatural rigor.

I'd give anything to be walking one day down a street in some city in the world and have a stranger come up to me and say they're finding it harder and harder to understand what I write. I'd love to hear this because it would allow me, for just a few seconds, to be Valéry and respond to their criticism with the very words that the writer addressed to his friend, the abbot and literary critic Henri Brémond, who scolded him for the same thing. Valéry looked the clergyman up and down and said what he had to realize was that he, Valéry, had not spent his life getting up between four and five in the morning to write a load of nonsense.

25

"Paris," I say to myself. "A stable, unmoving, intangible place."

Last night I woke up remembering the moment when I'd

said "Paris" the previous day and how I'd become so over-excited at the thought of Valéry, a rather cold intellectual figure who had nonetheless got me all fired up.

Last night—or, more precisely, at five in the morning; all I was missing was the shawl—I imagined ancient animal tracks, insect prints in the snow in Rome, lights and voids in the city of Reykjavík, cobwebs in the middle of the Sonoran Desert. And afterward I felt upset, as if I'd foreseen something I didn't know quite how to bring about, if indeed I ever could. And I ended up thinking about the "fantasy of the writer" that Barthes spoke of. The illusion, he said, that once reigned among certain young people in France and then practically disappeared when it became unusual to find an adolescent there who'd be impressed by a writer sitting in a café, or fantasize about being like him one day.

And Barthes remembered many young people of his generation who, dazzled by "the fantasy of the writer" as opposed to the work, aspired to that very fantasy and copied not the writer's work but his everyday habits, his way of strolling through the world—Barthes recalled—with a notebook in his pocket and a phrase in his head, "the way I imagined Gide traveling from Russia to the Congo, reading his classics and writing his notebooks in the dining car, waiting for the meals to be served; the way I actually saw him, one day in 1939, in the gloom of the Brasserie Lutétia, eating a pear and reading a book."

For Barthes, this outmoded fantasy of "wanting to be a writer" was misguided from the outset, "for what the fantasy imposes is the writer as we can see him in his private diary"; in other words, he made us see *the writer minus his work:* supreme form of the sacred: the mark and the void."

On the one hand, then, in those times Barthes was describing, there was the writer minus his work, reading a book in the Lutétia, left entirely in peace, but with some young man watching him from a distance, surely longing to eat the same pear, but little knowing that he'd simply have to sit down and write when the time for writing came.

And isn't that, coincidentally, what happened to me with Mastroianni when I was fifteen and saw him play the writer Pontano in Michelangelo Antonioni's *La notte*? Everything suggests I wanted to be like him, or rather, that I *wanted to be him,* overlooking the fact that to be him I had to write, first and foremost, and that it wasn't enough to "go about playing the writer." But back then I hadn't yet learned that writing also required you to "stop pretending to be a writer" and even, if the opportunity arose, to completely erase all traces of yourself from behind your words.

26

And so, on one side, we'd have Pontano, a pear in his hand and *minus the work;* just him, without so much as a knife for his fruit, the closest thing possible to the writer as fantasy. And then, on the other, a few "French writers," not always French, but all true writers, attentive to the *discipline de l'esprit,* which is ever unstable and moving, but ideal if what you want is not to settle—even if you're a French writer— anywhere, not even in Paris.

Cascais

Having lived in Paris unfits you for living anywhere,
including Paris.
—John Ashbery

1

After I finished the "Paris" section, which the reader has possibly just read, I went three years without writing anything at all, totally adrift. What's more, no sooner had I stopped writing than *things started happening to me*—a very strange development. It's not that things didn't happen to me before, but the things that started happening once I'd abandoned my desk all had something in common: they met every requirement for being turned into stories, and indeed they demanded it, almost crying out to be told.

And now here I am, once again. I sit back down at my desk as if no time had passed and leave behind all my railing against what can be narrated and what has been narrated, against narrative and plot. I also leave behind the "Paris" section, which for three years had me wiped out as a writer, perhaps because I tried to undertake a *biography of my style* to see where it would lead me, and it led me down a dead end.

It seems clear I was rather too hasty in my headlong rush into Paul Valéry's world, embarking on a wild goose chase in pursuit of aphorisms and ideas so as to avoid the *activity of storytelling,* for which, aside from my suspicion that it wasn't for me, I also felt thoroughly unqualified. But, who knows, perhaps what I've been calling my *Valerian breakdown* was actually more of a life-saving miracle: that epiphany, which came just in time, about where my admiration for Valéry was leading me, namely to the very place so wisely identified by Julien Gracq in one of his comments on that writer: "His drama was that of the ultra-rapid exhaustion of creative power through the exercise of analytical intelligence."

The "Paris" section was going to be the first chapter of a book, now definitively abandoned, which would have covered the story of my style in its entirety and which I planned to begin with the inevitable Nabokov quote: "The best part of a writer's biography is not the record of his adventures but the story of his style."

Nabokov's words couldn't have been closer to my own thoughts, but all my life I've been very indecisive, so I can't help telling myself that this marvelously modest line of Flaubert's could have worked just as well in its place: "And so I am going to resume my poor, dreary, tranquil existence in which sentences themselves are adventures."

My aim with the "Paris" section was precisely to avoid the classic banal record of a writer's adventures. But the *Valerian pages,* as I now refer to the final part of "Paris," put paid to that—perhaps, I'd even say in hindsight, for the best.

Blue skies in Barcelona this morning. On the radio, "Stumblin' In," a song that raises my spirits to such extraordinary heights that I'm convinced the feeling won't ever leave me. How strange, I think, for there to be music down the dead end, not to mention a way out. And in my current euphoric state, I feel able to describe the various events that led me from room to room, from door to door and all around the world, until I arrived at the *new* door that looks out, and indeed opens onto, these very pages.

2

One fine morning, not long after the section called "Paris" wiped me out as a writer, and having accepted an invitation to the Lisbon film festival from the Portuguese producer Paulo Branco, I found myself arriving in the Portuguese town of Cascais, overlooking the great blue expanse of the Atlantic.

As I stood on the sunlit terrace of the Miragem Hotel, before so much as putting down my suitcase, I recognized Jean-Pierre Léaud: the double of François Truffaut, the unforgettable Antoine Doinel in *The 400 Blows,* the charming young man in *Stolen Kisses,* and the not-so-charming young man in Godard's *Weekend.*

I didn't dare go over and accost him, thanks to my new-found insecurities ever since I'd stopped writing and become, to my mind, a nobody. And also because the actor, who had been the very embodiment of the most imaginative and gutsy movement of my generation, cut a truly terrifying figure—far more so than the other time I'd seen him, in Paris—staring intently out to sea, and because, what was more, it would have taken real courage to walk over there, as I wanted to do, and ask, I imagine with a mixture of respect and fear, if he'd mind me taking his photo.

My first instinct was to photograph him so as to have a souvenir of that glorious and—to me—deeply strange coincidence of coming face to face with the boy from *The 400 Blows,* with whom, more than half a century before, I'd so identified; most of all at the end of the movie, when, with the sea behind him, he looks straight into the camera.

You might be very unassuming, but your phone with its top-of-the-range camera certainly isn't, I imagined Léaud replying if I did indeed approach him to ask—in my most deferential voice—if I could trouble him for a photo. And so, cautious in the extreme, I didn't take a single step, instead simply staring at him, studying him from afar. Three yards from where I stood, David Cronenberg and Adam Thirlwell were sitting at a table, deep in conversation.

It seemed there was almost no one on the whole of that crowded terrace who wasn't a guest of the film festival. And I remember how, having been an avid reader of *Cahiers du Cinéma* in my youth, I was amazed to see, in one corner, a true legend from that time: the Polish director and screenwriter Jerzy Skolimowski.

However, given that everyone around me seemed to be at the top of their game, and meanwhile I was in the throes of a humiliating writer's block and burdened by a complex about having become a shameful nonentity, I felt completely incapable of talking to anyone, and suspected I'd go blank if I tried.

That day, on that terrace, I was gripped, as I so often have been, by conflicting emotions. Sometimes I'd think that my life in recent months, ever since "Paris" put me out of action, hadn't been so bad: I'd grown used to living in a series of identical days, days without writing, and which could be really quite marvelous, because, when I thought about it, they looked a lot like quiet endings to unimportant novels.

3

And then I realized I could go and speak to Adam Thirl-well, whom I not only knew but considered a friend. What was more, he had no way of knowing I'd been struck down by the Rimbaud syndrome from *Virtuosos of Suspense.*

I almost interrupted Thirlwell's conversation with David Cronenberg, best known to me as the director of *Spider,* a psychological thriller with a delirious feel, which, despite having nothing to do with Joyce, Beckett, or Dublin, inspired me to write—with its portrait of an insane young man caught up in a mental spiderweb in East London—a short story that, after it was published, ended up becoming the basis for my novel *Dublin Bay.*

I told Cronenberg and Thirlwell that I found Léaud's extreme seriousness so terrifying I didn't dare photograph him head on. And I remember very well how Thirlwell smiled and suggested that he pose in front of my state-of-the-art phone camera in such a position that Léaud, though tiny and very much in the background, would nonetheless end up, without even realizing it, inside the frame of the photo—the photo which I then took, and kept, and which I have beside me now as I write this.

Hours later, António Costa and Paulo Branco informed me that, quite aside from having captured Léaud in my photograph, I would have him in the next-door room to mine that night, but I didn't give it much thought. I had dinner in the hotel with Paulo Branco's young children and their friends, and then took the elevator up to the third floor, where I was staying.

By around midnight I was tucked up in bed and feeling

quite relaxed in my room, staring at the blank TV screen and listening to the gentle murmur of waves in the background. As I lay there, I was stubbornly racking my brain for ideas for an essay—I was still obsessed with making a return to writing and had a sense of how long my block would last— or, failing that, for ideas of how to fill my life with something and escape the sense of emptiness I'd begun to feel lurking nearby, threatening a return to those teenage years I spent wrestling with Nothingness, probably because nothing ever happened to me.

But I didn't honestly believe inspiration would strike. Deep down, what I wanted, and this would have been more than enough, was for the search itself—my alternative to counting sheep, which had never worked for me—to send me to sleep.

I was in bed and perfectly bereft of ideas, though also feeling quite relaxed in my room, as I wondered for the first time how I could possibly still believe that an essay would be my ticket out of writer's block. And that was when I heard Jean-Pierre Léaud's first fit of laughter. It was the very last thing I'd expected. Great guffaws that broke the silence in what I'd call a deliberately brash way, as if they had to be obscene to avoid any doubt that they were there and intended to prevent me from sleeping, or from concentrating on my increasingly unlikely future essay.

What on earth could have driven Léaud to laugh in such an uproarious way, bearing in mind how forbidding he'd seemed that morning on the terrace looking out to sea? Had he perhaps worked out that I was the same person he'd seen back in Paris on the terrace at Les Deux Magots and therefore begun to suspect, in the middle of the night, that I was in the neighboring room and so decided to laugh nonstop like a madman? But before I could rule out that harebrained hypothesis, the second round of laughter began; fainter now, but no less aggravating.

With no clues forthcoming as to what was going on, I instead turned to speculation and imagined Léaud was dreaming he was Nikolai Stepanovich Gumilev. In which case, I thought, I'll let him off, because he's probably deep in an anti-Leninist dream and because, moreover, he thinks he's the great Gumilev, about whom the only thing I know—and this is more than enough for me—is that he was murdered by Lenin's supporters. And apparently, all through his interrogation in the shadowy prosecutor's offices, and in the torture chamber, and in the winding corridors that led to the police van, and in that van which took him to his place of execution, and then there, in that place, where the earth was churned up by the heavy feet of a glum, gawky firing squad, the poet Gumilev never once stopped laughing.

It's well known that laughter is a sign of failed repression but perhaps less well known that Kafka's laughter, rising above any kind of repression, recalled the faint rustle of paper. It was precisely that tone, that persistent rustling, that was so mercilessly emitted that night, in the darkness of Cascais, by my neighbor's four hundred laughs—and lonely laughs, too, in his case, because everything suggested he was the only guest at that very private party in the next-door room.

And it was possibly that same rustling that made me imagine Léaud reenacting a real-life episode from interwar Prague, the one where the young Kafka couldn't contain his giggling fit during the official ceremony at which his boss, the president of the Workers' Accident Insurance Institute, appointed him as something like "the Institute's new drafting clerk."

As far as we know, it was a dicey moment for young Kafka, who'd only wanted to thank his boss—his friend's father and a symbolic stand-in for the emperor—for the promotion and instead had to watch as the scene unraveled, and with it his best intentions, because the harder he tried, the more calamitously he failed to contain his hysterical laughter.

4

I was imagining Jean-Pierre Léaud laughing, this time truly hysterically—lucky, I thought, that I'm only *imagining* these latest four hundred laughs—when I suddenly became aware of the deathly hush that had fallen over the Miragem Hotel, over my room, and even over the room next door. I took the opportunity to compose, or rather, to attempt to compose in my head, an aphorism about the uncertainty of my situation. I was almost there, albeit not entirely convinced, in large part because it sounded more and more like one of Lichtenberg's, if not exactly the same: "The fly that doesn't want to be swatted is most secure if it lights on the fly swatter."

And then the laughter came back, as if it wanted to laugh at me and my inchoate aphorism and essayistic endeavors, which were quite clearly going down the pan. This time the laughter was different, somewhat broken and softer than the kind I'd heard earlier, which had seemed more interested in reminding me of the faint rustle of paper. And for a moment I thought Léaud had a visitor.

5

As the night drew to a close, and when the laughter from the adjoining room had been silent for exactly an hour, I once again bemoaned my sleepless state. And since I could no longer blame Léaud, I began trying to see myself *from the outside,* as if I were looking into my room from the balcony. And at that precise moment, in that room overlooking the Atlantic, I ended up seeing myself for what I really was: a person reduced, by the uncontrollable forces of the dead of night, to a state of sheer terror, and what's more looking a fool of the uppermost cosmic order in my green striped pajamas that clashed so horrendously with the blue of the Atlantic.

I tried to turn my mind to other things, some of them no less ridiculous than my deplorable pajamas, and it seemed to me that if, after me thinking these things, a third wave of laughter broke out from my neighbor, I would no longer be able to shake the suspicion that he was laughing at my very thoughts, or at least, at what he thought I was thinking.

In the end I decided not to think about anything, to avoid a new wave. And I told myself that if Léaud really needed to laugh, it should at least be at something intended to be funny. I came up with a few lines to amuse myself and they turned out pretty dire: "It looks like I'm talking, and I'm not. It looks like it's about me, and it's not. I'm so lonesome, a lonesome pair of pajamas, and I could just die on the spot." I learned it by heart as if I might be called upon to perform it right there in the middle of the night, and it struck me that the "I could just die on the spot" revealed writer's block to be the least of my problems. Because I wasn't referring to dying for love, or for my country, or even for no reason at all, but rather to dying from the shame of wearing pajamas that clashed so horribly with the ocean. Surely only an idiot would come up with something like that?

Good grief, I thought, I'd better raise the tone a little, so that if Léaud does laugh again, it's at something more substantial. And I constructed a deliberately reflective sentence at top speed. Still no laughter. I played at putting myself in the shoes of the poor president of the Workers' Accident Insurance Institute in Prague, and imagined him giving a speech that was just as painful as the one that had tickled Kafka so much, only relevant to the here and now. I pictured him saying: "What changes in our perception of the world have we witnessed in recent times? Have we been able to detect any? One thing is clear, or so I believe: all our philosophical systems and structures, technological ones included, have been developed to create some sort of meaning, which, as we all know, doesn't exist."

The devilish cackle of Kafka's uncle, now transformed into a shepherd, filled my entire room. In the room next door, a deep, suspicious silence.

My mind wandered then—as if, like a consummate sleepwalker, I'd stepped out onto my balcony—to some words of Herman Melville's whose context I didn't know, and little did it seem to matter, because, unlike that exasperating "I would prefer not to," this phrase was all the better for its lack of tangible textual fabric; it was a phrase with the good grace— as I saw it then—to remain unexplained for all eternity.

"The malicious Devil is forever grinning in upon me, holding the door ajar."

At this rate, I thought, I'll never get to sleep.

(Third fit of unhinged laughter from next door.)

6

If there's one episode in my life that has always felt completely *unnarratable,* it's the one that took place in Almería, in a military camp, a year before I first landed in Paris. All of a sudden I noticed—and what follows, being so unnarratable, and therefore so difficult to convey, is no more than a loose approximation—some flashing lights that made me think of nodes connecting the past and the present, and also of interlinked points in time and space, whose topology, I realized then, I would never understand but between which, I felt, with a remote but conceivable certainty, the so-called living and the so-called dead could move, and in that way encounter one another.

I've often returned to this episode, sometimes after hearing of other people's experiences that have reminded me, albeit hazily, of my own. The closest thing to this story I want to tell, but feel incapable of describing as fully as I'd like, I found in an interview with W. G. Sebald in which he explained that he'd gone to a London museum to see two paintings and that behind him, also looking at them, was a couple conversing in a Central European language (Hungarian or Polish, he couldn't say which), a strange-looking couple who seemed almost from a different time, and not only because of the way they were dressed. Five hours later, the writer had to travel to one of the outermost Underground stations in London, which, as we know, is a city of more than ten million inhabitants. There was no one but him on the platform as he awaited the train—except for the couple from the museum. Sebald concluded that coincidences weren't in fact chance events but that there was a relationship some-

where that glinted, every now and then, through a threadbare piece of cloth.

7

But did I really want to go back to telling stories in an
age when the art of wandering and pondering through the
many regions of that threadbare piece of cloth—which I had
no problem identifying wholeheartedly with literature—was
now to be found in total liquidation, supplanted by the sordid ambitions of careerists, the impossible sincerity of certain nonfiction, the third-rate hacks with no literary experience, and so many other narrative trends sponsored by
Usury International?

Was it all so very hopeless? Well, it certainly wasn't time
to break out the champagne, which made me think the most
sensible route was that of moderate despair. One example of
that moderation: to boost my resolve as I drifted away from
writing, all I needed was to read a news headline from New
York saying that Fran Lebowitz grew more renowned with
every book she didn't write.

That was enough to keep me happy for the rest of the
day. Because I was happy, and all the more so since I'd begun
to suspect that the opposite path—that of not being happy—
could mean ending up like my friend and colleague, poor
Kurt Kobel, a writer from Leipzig who never hid how lost
he was and who, not long ago, had written to me in Barcelona from Bern: a heartbreaking letter—and enormously
propitious, I thought as I read it—encouraging me not to despair. Kobel wrote it from the house, now a museum, where

Einstein's first son had been born and where Einstein—no thanks to the pet cat who messed up all the papers containing his most promising equations—formulated the theory of relativity.

Kobel had gone to that house, he told me with doleful humor, to see if some of Einstein's genius might rub off on him. And in case the previous lines hadn't been depressing enough, he ended that dreadful letter with the claim that the current age was like a pot of water we've left bubbling away, full of people who don't realize we might all dissolve in it, this being the true spirit of the times.

Ever since I received that letter, the spirit of the times has been a constant presence in my life, seeking to drown me, to plunge me into despair, and even inciting me to kill, in a moment of extreme madness, any occupant of a neighboring hotel room who might appear to be sneering at the thoughts that come into my head during my search for metaphysical sheep.

And with that thought, I pressed my right ear to the wall separating me from the adjoining room. I heard nothing, and ended up wondering what kind of fright I'd intended to give Léaud with my murderous musings, when deep down, no matter how strong my suspicions, I knew he couldn't possibly be listening in on what I was thinking.

Since I didn't hear so much as a nervous titter—I'd intended to give him a warning, to scare him to death, so to speak—or notice any sign of life from his room, I understood, and accepted, that Léaud could have no possible connection to what I was thinking.

And just then—good grief—a fourth wave of laughter broke out.

8

I needed to distract myself from the tension created by that stubbornly recurring laughter, and so, as I was trying to get some sleep, I invented "the *Je est un autre* game," which was essentially a shock tactic to avoid having a terrible time when people inevitably began to ask what on earth had happened to make me stop writing. *Je est un autre* allowed me to be *another* without ceasing to be me; that is, it gave me the chance to answer the question of why I wasn't writing with a line from whichever worldly figure I was reminded of by the questioner's demeanor. For example, if a reader approached me one day in the street to ask if I'd worked out why I wasn't writing, and the way they phrased that question made me think of the ones put to Neil Armstrong on his return from the Moon—everyone wanted to know if he'd worked out why we're here or where we come from—I would pretend to be that other person, in this case Armstrong, and give the same answer they tended to give, bamboozling the nosy inquisitor. I'd reply that I was an engineer who, along with many other people, had succeeded in getting man to the Moon, but that I wouldn't presume to respond to questions that fell beyond my remit.

I had no way of knowing, as I lay there in bed, that the opportunity to play my first round of *Je est un autre* would come so soon, indeed the very next day, at Lisbon airport, because I'd have to return urgently to Barcelona. Just as I was about to board the plane, deeply upset by some news from my brother, I ran into an old girlfriend, Lisa Barinaga, who pounced on me and asked, with barely any preamble, what I was currently writing and if it was about "lovely" Lisbon.

Lovely? That wasn't the word, I thought. I could have let that adjective and even her question slide, but I was in no mood to suffer such inanities in silence. And since Lisa Barinaga was particularly keen on modern art—even her dress and voice had something modern about them—I responded with the exact words Duchamp spoke to the sculptor Naum Gabo when Gabo asked why he'd stopped painting. "Mais que voulez-vous?" Duchamp replied, spreading wide his arms, "je n'ai plus d'idées." (What do you expect? I've no more ideas.)

Lisa Barinaga was speechless, perhaps because of my swift response and the way I'd spread wide my arms. I was even tempted to apologize. But the devil in me egged me on, and I made Duchamp, whom, at that moment, I had quite clearly become, utter something more theatrical still:

"What's a man to do, Lisa? It's not even a sentence a day now. I finished the 'Paris' section and it left me broken, with no *mind's eye* and unable to go on, with only my chess and my steps on the Moon."

I thought she might ask me to explain the mind's eye, the "Paris" section, the chess, and the steps on the Moon, and perhaps also exactly what I understood by "go on," but instead, to my surprise, she advised me to bear in mind that long-held emotions were always strange, and when they weren't even *my* emotions, as was obviously the case here—after all, she knew me pretty well and felt sure I'd been speaking as somebody else—she could only find them painfully embarrassing.

And with that, she took off, or, more precisely, took her leave of me, a lost Duchamp, defeated on the chessboard of life, not to mention the chessboard of the Moon, and without a right of reply.

That didn't go so well, I said to myself. I think the game still needs some fine-tuning.

9

It was on hearing the fifth round of laughter from my neighbor, that icon of my generation, that I thought: How could anyone get through life shouldering a burden like this—the burden of speaking out against novels with plots? And later on, this time sans laughter, I thought: Clearly I'll never find out what the hell all this is: the world, this spherical rock upon which we hurtle along at top speed and without a driver, on the maddest of rides, where one day we're lying beside our love and the next in the cold, hard ground.

I thought: The part about Billie Holiday is the only thing I'd save from *Virtuosos of Suspense.* Because I still love that hint of self-destruction that spread through Billie's art and is so common among extraordinarily talented people—Cézanne, Morandi, Nabokov, Borges—who, precisely because of it, tend to be doomed to relive their highest moments of inspiration for all eternity.

I thought: Right now I should stand up, that is, *raise myself up* and at least write one line, even just the first line of a letter; if I can't sleep, I could at least try writing something sublime, never mind that I don't write anymore . . . .

(A strange noise in the adjoining room, as if something invisible and therefore indescribable were stirring)

I thought: Were I to return to writing one day, my next book would have an invisible subject. It would be clear to the reader that I never lost sight of my subject, but nor would I really go into it, instead treating it as implicit and indescribable. I wouldn't even name it, but rather let it glide over my readers, hovering above the solid crux of the book, invisible but nonetheless omnipresent, precisely because it was indescribable.

I thought: Dance, rise higher, perhaps even a sting. Yes, I'd be quite prepared to launch myself onto the other balcony and deliver a sting.

(Laughter, which for a moment it seemed would never stop)

I thought: I wouldn't mind hearing the laughter again right away, for it to return, with its mystery intact, secret and irrepressible, and more tolerable than life, with dead time or traffic jams, forging on like a train in the night, pure rustling paper.

(Laughter and a hacking cough)

I thought: So poetry isn't his thing, though he seems to find it amusing.

I thought: Go out onto your balcony and try to see what he's doing on his.

I thought: What if what I see from my balcony turns out to be an entirely describable god, man, or beast, with the hideous face of a neighboring Frenchman, mouthless yet laughing, and with shiny dark circles under his squinty eyes?

(Deathly silence)

I thought: What if my neighbor's an elephant?

(More silence)

I thought: It's becoming a real mystery when the laughter will come and when it will disappear.

(More silence)

I didn't think twice. I had to take action, so I went out

onto my balcony, but from there I could see nothing of the adjoining room, not even whether the light was on.

The typical divider made of tall fake grass obstructed any possible view of the adjoining balcony. Instead, I was met with the terrifying sight of a spider some two inches wide, perched right there in the grass. I remembered how I'd once seen a bird-eating tarantula in Venezuela and been quite shaken up, and later hadn't been able to get it out of my head. But I was more shaken by this spider, simply because it seemed so thoroughly out of place there, between my neighbor's balcony and mine.

I hadn't expected it, in other words, even if it did fall rather short of a bird-eating tarantula. And I even ended up taking a step back, though I soon regretted that hasty reaction, because the spider, it turned out, was as fake as the grass. A charming, witty touch laid on by the hotel management for its valued clientele?

10

By then I'd gone a while without hearing any laughter, but also without sleeping a wink. And it was torture, being paralyzed not only as a writer but also there before the ocean, trapped inside the night. And I thought about Liz, a friend from Barcelona who'd recently gone through a similar kind of torture, only, in her case, in a hospital. Liz had told me that, at the height of the uncertainty, when she hadn't known if she would live or die, what she felt wasn't fear but a vast, sweeping emptiness. At night she would lie awake and anxiously await the coming morning, as if the first light of dawn would save her.

And just as I was starting to notice the first signs of dawn, my phone rang. It was my brother, sounding terribly upset, calling to tell me that our father had just died. Although he had been very ill, neither of us had expected the end to come so soon. And, despite being inherently indecisive, I can say with total certainty that, had it not been for the unexpected dawn news, I wouldn't now be remembering so much about that icon of my generation, Truffaut's alter ego, and his four hundred laughs that night—but then again, I doubt I'd have forgotten it completely, because we always hold grudges against those who, for whatever reason, come between us and our sleep.

When my brother called, I was lost in a complex network of thoughts and speculations, each as gloomy as the last, and from among which, at a certain point, one voice in particular stood out, with a force all of its own, telling me that for a very long time, indeed for years now, it had had an idea. And since I've had this idea for a long time, the voice repeated, obsessively, over and over, I can see how constricted I've been, how confined, locked up, and smothered. I'm better now, it added, and ready to start again. For a long time, years, I've had an idea . . . . And since I've had this idea for a long time . . . .

It always finished with the same words:

"I'm better now."

It was precisely then that I received the distressing phone call that left me completely flustered and unsure how to react. I promised my brother I'd be in Barcelona the very next day, and after hanging up, I let my mind drift, aware that everything—my room and the room next door, the hotel and the ocean—had gone the way of the infinite tedium of Robert Walser's courtyard during siesta hours: "deserted like a foursquare eternity." An extraordinary image, because how better to describe the link between sleep and the suspension of time.

The most curious thing about the situation was that, in the old courtyard of life that was that room overlooking the Atlantic, time, against all odds and flouting any notion of suspension, didn't want to stop even for a second; quite the opposite, because there was no lull in proceedings whatsoever. A few minutes later, as if wanting to join forces with the feelings of shock and disorientation that had left me so powerless, a tinny, imperious voice *took over* my room, warning "all guests" that a fire had broken out in the hotel and advising us to vacate the building in a calm and orderly manner.

I couldn't see any fire from my window. Of course, I didn't have a view of the hotel's rear wall, which faced onto the coast road. I couldn't think where that tinny voice was coming from, and for a few seconds I had the bizarre and foolish idea that it was coming from my smartphone. What's more, it seemed as if the sadness that flowed from my brother's call had found its means of prolongation in that alarm.

Unsure what was happening or what to do, I stepped out onto my balcony, in the daylight this time. The spider was completely unfazed. There's nothing like not being real to keep life simple, I thought. And then I took a moment to study the spider's design, which hovered somewhere between meticulous Paleolithic detail and the most extreme, electric modernity—a perfect combination. All was calm. I didn't hear a single cry for help. No one was running, no one was screaming and throwing themselves off the side of the building. It was a glorious sunrise; the ocean had never been bluer. All was peace in that first hour of the day.

And I remembered a similar experience I'd had years before, also in Portugal, when I'd been in a restaurant on Rua das Janelas Verdes in Lisbon on the day of the Twin Towers attack and my father had called from Barcelona to tell me World War Three had broken out. Come home, he practically ordered, as if deep down reproaching me for spending so much of my time gallivanting around the world and so little of it, of late, in my hometown.

That Tuesday, after lunch, I left the restaurant believing the whole world had gone up in flames. Outside, the sky—glimpsed through the unforgettable soaring palm trees of Lisbon's Museum of Ancient Art neighborhood—was so blue and serene, and the calm of the Rua das Janelas Verdes so immense, that it was impossible to imagine a crisis of such magnitude anywhere on Earth.

11

My state-of-the-art phone was terrific, but it could also be deceptive because, however ultramodern, it didn't have, for example, an alarm app for people staying in hotels. When it finally sank in that there could be a fire four yards away, in my very corridor, I bolted from my room without a second thought. But once outside, I remembered I was still in my pajamas and stopped dead. There was no one around, but all the same I sheepishly retreated to my room to get changed, only to be struck by the realization that if there really was a fire, wasting my time on such nonsense could very well cost me my life, and so back out I went in my pajamas, though not rushing this time, as if going slowly could somehow make the green stripes of my atrabilious outfit less visible.

I would soon learn that the alarm had been triggered by

the most minimal of fires in the hotel kitchen, whose appliances were perhaps too high-tech for their own good. But to find that out, I would have to drag my feet—or my slippers, to be precise—down three stories to reception, which was no easy task. First, on leaving my room, I shuffled along the corridor to the third-floor elevator, where I saw, also waiting to go down and completely ignoring each other, Lucy Sante and Jean-Pierre Léaud.

A Mexican song, "Ojitos Negros," was playing in the background. Nice tune, I thought, but I'd better concentrate on saving my life. I'd already said hello to Lucy Sante at the previous day's lunch organized on Guincho Beach, when I'd congratulated her on *The Other Paris,* that wonderful book about the city's underworld.

Since I was still some way away from where Sante and Léaud stood waiting, I began to wonder as I approached what I'd say to the former—given I'd already congratulated her on Guincho—and then, were I to get the chance, what I'd say to the latter, that icon of my generation and the direct cause of my exhausted, sleep-deprived state.

I was still a few yards away when they both decided at once, though without conferring, to give up on the elevator, perhaps thinking that by the time it did appear, it would be ablaze. I saw them positively slink through a side door leading onto a back staircase but overestimated my own speed and reached the door long after them, meaning that when I called down from the top of the steps to ask Jean-Pierre Léaud why he'd been laughing so much in the night, his response came from far below me:

"Pas du tout."

I took this to mean that he hadn't been laughing at all.

Or that he hadn't slept remotely well. Or that I was the one who'd done all the laughing and was therefore now asking if *I'd* bothered *him*. And right there, at the top of the stairs, knowing I was free to think whatever I wanted and didn't have to answer to anyone, I told myself—this was my modest, secret revenge—that Léaud had been laughing all night at the way humanity had taken such great pains in recent centuries to print so many phrases.

In short, not having received the explanation I'd hoped for from Léaud, I saddled him with that print-related peeve and got back to the more pressing matter of returning to Barcelona that night.

And then, as I made my way down the stairs, I wondered if there'd ever been a satisfactory explanation for anything. Because, thinking about it, has anyone ever seen fit to explain why the universe contains something rather than nothing, and why one day the opposite will be true and there'll be nothing where before there was something? And who, then, will remember how, throughout the centuries, the Sun was mistaken for the supreme deity? Or perhaps there was no misunderstanding at all and the Sun, so revered by so many civilizations, has always been just what our ancestors suspected?

After this last question, I paused on the second-floor landing to observe how the potential fire had made me think about the Sun. And what with all this pausing and observing, I reached the ground floor some time after Lucy Sante and Jean-Pierre Léaud. At reception, where the staff seemed sick and tired of responding to inquiries, they told me that nothing was wrong and it had been a false alarm from the kitchen. I asked them to call me a taxi to the airport, but it was as if they hadn't heard. By now I was in a real state; it seemed the pajamas were stopping everyone from bothering to listen to me. Or that I couldn't go to the airport because I was wearing pajamas. My father has died, I tried again, and it was me who set fire to the kitchen, in protest against the raucous goings-on in the room next door I was forced to put up with last night.

They asked me to repeat all that more slowly. My father has died and I want a taxi, I said, somewhat calmer. To the airport, I added. And I will always remember the moment that followed, when I took a long, slow look around me. Jean-Pierre Léaud was nowhere to be seen—he'd probably gone off to print some more laughter. As for Lucy Sante, she'd even managed to squeeze in a bit of sunbathing and order breakfast. When our eyes met from afar, she gave me an icy cold smile, as if she'd hated how I'd praised her on Guincho Beach.

"Nice pajamas," someone murmured.

And I preferred not to turn around, lest it be Léaud twisting the knife even further.

Montevideo

1

There's a brilliant Julio Cortázar story in which the adjoining room in a hotel plays a fundamental role. It's called "The Sealed Door," belongs as much to the world of fiction as it does to real life, and takes place in the city of Montevideo, in Uruguay.

And so when, not long after my father's funeral, an opportunity arose to visit that city, my first thought after accepting the invitation was of that locked door behind a closet in the hotel room where Cortázar had set "The Sealed Door."

For years I'd wanted to visit the site of that fictional story, to see the closet and the door behind it, that sealed door that was so mythical to me, and try to find out what happened when a person stepped into a fictional space that also existed in the real world or, put another way, into a space in the real world that would be nothing without a fictional world, and vice versa, and so on ad infinitum.

Cortazár's story couldn't be more closely linked to narrative trend number three and the fertile terrain of those who seem as though they're going to tell you everything but always "leave a loose thread in the story." And I felt very interested in that "loose thread" left by Cortázar, convinced as I was that I would spare no effort when the time came to attempt—most wishful of wishful thinking—to "make it mine."

Indeed, "The Sealed Door" formed part of the very core of my lifelong obsessions, though I'd never seen it with my own eyes. So the invitation to visit Montevideo, from a Catalan man by the name of Sirés, came as excellent news, especially since at that point, having given up writing, I had more time on my hands for traveling to another part of the world.

And despite being so indecisive, I was almost certain that, considering the personal circumstances I was up against at that time, the trip to Uruguay would save me from the risk of becoming a total wreck.

Two personal circumstances were affecting me more than the others. First, the long, painful repercussions of my father's death. Second, the void I had to struggle through each day, especially in the mornings, when in the past I'd always written, and which suddenly, now that I'd stopped, were spent staring stupidly at the insects' comings and goings and regretting my drastic decision to close any door that might have led me back to writing fiction.

For just one week, I pushed back against my inertia and began getting up at four or five in the morning, always with a shawl around my shoulders and the idea and hope of overcoming that arguably ridiculous writer's block brought on by the "Paris" section. Though evidently I could think of no better way to overcome it than by copying Valéry's shawl and schedule, which surprised even me, because I realized it only served to show how thoroughly lost I was in the world. But then, we all have the right to dream, and also to get things wrong. In the words of George Steiner: "What interests me are the errors, the act of passion, the errors one makes when taking risks. Good heavens, how awful, the desire never to make a mistake!"

And, whatever happened, I wasn't yet ready to give in, and would dream, timidly, of repeating the journey of that "modern-day intellectual Odysseus through the labyrinth of his own closed-off mind" (Sánchez Robayna on Valéry), although, quite predictably, the most I achieved was to find a phrase—a single phrase over five early mornings—that I deemed worthy of being typed up onto my computer.

But the phrase said something that within a matter of hours I had to delete because it was too close to a line from Valéry's *Cahiers:*

> "I recoil in horror from any label that people want to give me."

That setback proved fatal and reduced me to silence, and I heard with some unease the sound of a door which, as it closed, sent me right back to the first of the narrative trends that I myself had come up with.

And precisely because I felt I was back where I'd started, I took to drifting endlessly around Barcelona, thinking now and then that all that was missing was for me to start kicking stones down Paseo de Gracia or to make my way to the very same Paseo de San Juan from my childhood and reencounter the void, the exact center of my life's geography, that place where nothing ever happened.

Besides, given the suffocating circumstances of my life as a born-again illiterate, I began to sense that in Montevideo I would be able to live, for a few days, in a manner not unlike the way I sometimes listen to the radio: waiting for the next song, the song that might change the course of, if not my life, then at least my morning.

"The Sealed Door" begins with a description of the Hotel Cervantes in downtown Montevideo; the place where Petrone, the protagonist of this story told to us in the third person, is going to stay. Someone recommended the hotel to him, and he chose a room on the second floor. The narrator, who describes the hotel as "gloomy, quiet, almost deserted," repeatedly mentions the silence within, a silence that makes even the slightest sound seem cacophonous. Petrone's room, we learn, doesn't get much light or air, and the room next door—the manager informs him when he arrives—is occupied by a single woman who's out at work all day and returns there only to sleep.

On the first night, after a busy day's work, Petrone comes back to his room exhausted and quickly falls asleep. When he wakes up, "in those first minutes that still contain the dregs of night and sleep," he's bothered by the sound of a baby crying, though he doesn't think anything of it.

On the second night, Petrone takes a closer look at his room and finds that the closet has been positioned in front of a door leading to the adjoining room. Again, he soon falls asleep, but then he hears the child crying once more, this time perfectly clearly, and feels sure the sound is coming from whatever lies behind the sealed door, thus confirming that he heard rightly the first night and the crying hadn't been part of his dream. Then he thinks that there couldn't possibly be a baby in the single woman's room. He manages to go back to sleep but soon wakes up again because this time, in addition to the child crying, he can hear the woman trying to console it.

The next morning, in a foul mood after such a bad night's

sleep, he speaks to the manager about the problem with the baby but is assured that there are no children in the hotel. On the third night, however, the crying is there again, though Petrone almost doesn't believe his ears, as if the manager's words were more credible than the sound itself.

The climax of the story comes when Petrone moves the closet and reveals the sealed door. Not content with merely banging on the wall, he mimics the child's irritating crying, he whines and wails, listening all the while to the woman's frantic footsteps on the other side.

The next day, still half asleep, he hears the voices of the hotel owner and the woman downstairs in reception. At ten o'clock, on the way out of his room, he sees some suitcases and a trunk by the elevator. And when he goes down, the manager informs him that the lady will be leaving the hotel that very afternoon. Outside, Petrone becomes light-headed and can't stop thinking about the baby. He feels guilty about the poor woman leaving and considers going back to apologize, but stops himself. That night, on returning to the hotel, he's very uneasy in his room. Perhaps he's missing the little tot's crying, he thinks sarcastically. The silence gradually becomes unbearable; it feels thick and oppressive, and he finds it even gives him trouble sleeping. Later on he hears the child crying again and realizes the woman was doing a good job of consoling it.

3

When I read, some years ago, that Beatriz Sarlo had described that sealed door as "the exact place where the fantastical bursts into Cortázar's story," I felt all the more inclined to travel to Montevideo one day and stand before that "exact place."

"One day I'll go to Montevideo and look for the room on the second floor of the Cervantes Hotel, and it will be a real-life journey to the exact place of the fantastical, perhaps the exact place of strangeness itself," I'd even written at one point, with rather more fireworks than conviction, though by now it's a well-known fact that a lack of conviction can lead us, whether we expect it or not, to conviction itself.

But my interest began in earnest only when I read the Vlady Kociancich essay in which she mentions the fantastical coincidence between "The Sealed Door" and "A Journey, or the Immortal Wizard," a story written by Bioy Casares over almost the same days when Cortázar wrote his, and with a strikingly similar plot.

Kociancich said that, while the chance resemblance between the plots was strange enough, the presence of so many other coincidences made it even stranger. Cortázar's Petrone and Bioy's narrator had the same profession and traveled to the same city, Montevideo (on the *Vapor de la Carrera,* the legendary steamship that set out from Buenos Aires at ten at night and reached its destination the next morning), and both were due to check into the same gloomy, quiet hotel.

"Petrone liked things about the Hotel Cervantes that wouldn't have suited other people," Cortázar writes.

"I could have sworn I'd told the taxi driver: 'To the Cervantes Hotel.' How many times, in the early hours, have I gazed, with a heavy soul, through the bathroom window overlooking the gardens, at a lone tree, a pine, which stands on the same block as the hotel," says Bioy's narrator, who is taken aback to find his taxi pulling up outside the Hotel La Alhambra.

But the coincidences don't stop there. An almost identical melancholy view from the bathroom is mentioned at the beginning of both stories. And both protagonists are woken by the nocturnal voices of guests in the adjoining rooms: in the Cortázar, it's a child's enigmatic crying from behind a sealed door hidden by a closet that stops Petrone from sleeping, while the failed Don Juan in Bioy's story has to put up with a couple who copulate incessantly.

Bioy Casares brought up this strange matter of the coincidences in some remarks he made in the eighties: "As for Cortázar, I can tell you that, while he was in France and I was in Buenos Aires, we wrote an identical story. The action began on the *Vapor de la Carrera,* as it was called then. The protagonist was going to the Cervantes Hotel in Montevideo, a hotel that almost nobody has heard of. And from that point on, it was similar at every stage, which pleased us both very much."

And Cortázar, who had always spoken of the magical power of Montevidean hotels, said in an interview: "I wanted the atmosphere of the Cervantes Hotel to be there in the story, because in a way it encapsulates a lot of things about Montevideo for me. There was the character of the manager, that statue that stands (or stood) in the lobby—a replica of Venus—and also the general ambience of the hotel. I don't know who it was that recommended the Cervantes to me, where there was indeed a poky little room. Between the bed, the desk, and the large closet covering the sealed door, there was barely any space left to move."

4

I remember the exact afternoon in Barcelona when I learned, while surfing the Net, that the Hotel Cervantes in

Montevideo, located on Calle Soriano (the same street where Mario Levrero had his secondhand bookshop), between Calles Convención and Andes, still existed, which meant, for one thing, that the "poky little room" and the closet covering the sealed door were probably also still there.

I did some more research—as much as a person can manage from home—and it looked as if the hotel continued to be "gloomy" and "quiet," though it wasn't clear if it was as quiet as it used to be. In the basement, I read, were the remains of what had once been the stage of the Cervantes Theater and was now a parking lot. And the Grand Orient of Mixed Universal Freemasonry had, in "recent times," held its Sixth Great Assembly at the hotel, "brought off amid a great deal of hard work, and presided over by fraternity, calm, tolerance, and mutual respect."

One thing was clear: the hotel hadn't been renovated, so there was reason to believe that everything was still as it had been in Cortázar's story, although Fridays and Saturdays were rather busier than before thanks to the "wife swaps" attended by numerous swingers, who were apparently "gaining ground in Montevidean society, though losing it where the law is concerned."

I remember thinking: a wife swap is a kind of parallel narrative to the plot swap in Bioy's and Cortázar's stories. And when I read on a young Montevidean woman's blog, which clearly had nothing to do with "The Sealed Door," that the hotel's telephone number was 900-7991 and that the place was "a big deal in the swinging world, even though it's old and run-down, and my cousin told me she once went with her boyfriend and spotted a cockroach, so obviously she went to reception to ask for their money back," I wondered who would have been on duty that night, feeling quite certain it couldn't have been the manager who swore blind to Petrone that there was no baby in the hotel. Because if it had been, I thought, he would surely have denied the eminently contestable presence of a cockroach.

Was the Tower of Panoramas far from there? Years earlier, for the Barcelona magazine *El Viejo Topo,* I'd written an article about the tower—my first ever piece on a literary topic, and whose greatest merit had been to reveal in me a knack for slipping poetry into the pages of a political magazine. That alone would have granted the Tower of Panoramas a special place in my life, but then, some time after my article was published, I developed a separate fascination with it after learning more about the highly avant-garde world of that building overlooking the River Plate.

Even though I'd never set foot inside it, the tower was the thing I most admired and even felt I knew best in Montevideo, aside from Cortázar's sealed door. I'd looked at it several times online—something that, due to the lack of available resources, I'd never been able to do with the sealed door.

With its panoramic views of the Río de la Plata, the tower, as you'd expect, was not what it used to be, because the range of panoramas visible at the beginning of the century had been considerably reduced. What's more, the cramped little room on the tower's flat roof, where the "lunatics' salon" used to convene, had been emptied, leaving just four whitewashed walls, the same walls that had witnessed the poetic revolution led by the young and brilliant Julio Herrera y Reissig, a radical poet who seemed to have a reputation for both morphine addiction and revolutionizing Latin American literature. His family lived in the house underneath the tower, and he spent his nights on the rooftop, where he met with the rest of the group, that legendary, combative coterie: at once a kind of "savage detectives" *avant la lettre* and the beating heart of Latin American literary modernism.

At the time, only Valle-Inclán in Spain noticed the revolutionary impact of that Uruguayan poet who, from his mythical tower, anticipated all the avant-gardes and even, I think, the concave mirrors on Cat Alley in Madrid, which were already contained in those visionary verses that gave Herrera y Reissig a certain prominence at the time: "Spectral reality / passes through the tragic / and murky magic lantern / of my spectral reason."

The Tower of Panoramas, which is still there on the rooftop, albeit now with fewer panoramas, I murmur, is perhaps the exact place of my spectral reality. I murmur this and then allow the Río de la Plata—which I think the Uruguayans call the Mar de la Plata, a sea rather than a river, because from Montevideo you can't see the other bank—to slowly flood my bookish memory: the novel, for example, by Alexandre Dumas père, who described in *Montevideo, or the New Troy,* without ever having been to Uruguay, the brutal conflict that took place there, the seven-year siege of heroic Montevideo, a war in the style of modern-day Iraq, with federalist Shiites and unitarian Sunnis engaged in a dreadful, cruel, and endless struggle that's largely incomprehensible to Europeans.

5

For years I engaged in a kind of secret *saudade,* a strange overseas longing, a wistfulness about a place I had never been and wasn't sure I'd ever have the chance to go. That place was Montevideo. I became a fan of the poetry of Idea Vilariño, who was born in that city in 1920, ten years after Herrera y Reissig's death. And I never spoke a truer word than when I say that, as I read her, I often had the feeling I'd reached the center of the world. So much so that I came to associate the extraordinary pleasure I derived from Vilariño's poetry with the Tower of Panoramas, the spectral, poetic cenacle of that gathering of lunatics about which, at one point in time, I spent all my days trying to learn as much as I possibly could. The room where they met was three yards long and two wide, and the walls were covered in photos (it was the one of Mallarmé that always caught my eye), mostly pictures cut out of magazines. The only furnishings were "a miserable table and two rheumatic chairs." And hanging up in a very visible place: a fez and a pair of rusty foils.

The flat roof offered the most sweeping of panoramas: to the south, the brownish river; to the north, the mass of urban construction; to the east, the ragged coastline with its magnificent breakers and, beyond that, the cemetery and the curve of Estanzuela, all the way to the white milepost of the Punta Carretas Lighthouse; to the west, more river landscape, the port scattered with steamers, and above it all, the hill neighborhood of Cerro, with its slate-colored peak and rickety lime and terra-cotta houses . . . .

Sometimes, at night, I visited Montevideo in my imagination. And I found it quite amazing how that cramped little room inside that ingenious and almost villagey viewing station had been the origin of the literary revival of Uruguay and much of the Spanish-speaking world. As I thought about that, and analyzed the extent of the longing contained in those words, I came to realize that I now had a more than genuine need to set foot in that poky little room.

And then, at dawn, after my investigations into that far-away city, I would generally take my leave of it with some verses by the great Idea Vilariño, herself an expert in farewells, as was her beloved Juan Carlos Onetti, to whom she said goodbye in poem after poem, just as she did to the Darío she so admired: "Poor Rubén you believed / in all those things / glory sex poetry/ and sometimes America / and then you died / and now you're dead / dead."

6

One night in Barcelona, I was walking very slowly down a street thinking about how there are places in the world, like the Tower of Panoramas, where great things have happened, though nowadays nobody would think it possible; places that give no indication of how pivotal they were in their day. Places where changes of global importance occurred, and yet when people see them now—the tower is a deserted little room—they would never imagine that they had once been among the supreme forms of the sacred.

I carried on walking very slowly down that Barcelona street. And a mild fit of madness, that is, a well-controlled fit, made me think I was a ghost. I began to walk in a zigzag. There was no one around, which made my skewed trajectory all the easier. And then suddenly my phone rang, and I returned to the real world, and my ghost-life came to an end. A gravelly voice addressed me from Montevideo, reminding me that I'd been invited to visit the city and seeking confirmation that, as I'd already told them, I was indeed planning to go. I stopped walking so as to concentrate on my answer, to make sure no absurd misunderstanding somehow led me to miss out on that trip I was so keen to take. The person talking was Sirés, and he was informing me that he needed my confirmation so that he could finalize the Centro Cultural de España's events program, which he oversaw.

Yes, I said, I wasn't backing out. He went on to explain more about where he worked, and as he did so, I couldn't stop thinking about the fact he was called Sirés, because although I hadn't heard that name in a very, very long time, it was vaguely familiar to me, having been the name of one of my father's best friends, and also one whose memory was most lost to the years, a person I never knew much about (my mother loathed him); the most I'd ever learned was that he had a reputation for being the fancy man of certain ticket clerks at cinemas across the city. "The box-office king," my mother always called him, with undisguised contempt.

Three weeks later, I had just landed in Montevideo, and before we'd even left the airport I asked Sirés if he had any connection—I knew he'd say no, it was completely impossible—to my father's friend, the fancy man—I stressed the detail to be sure he'd heard—of certain box-office girls in Barcelona. He was taken aback.

"Box-office girls?"

It was as if I'd said the strangest thing in the world. Even his voice suddenly changed, and stopped sounding so gravelly. No connection whatsoever, he replied, adding that he had no idea what I was talking about, not least because his whole family was from Àger, in the Noguera region of Lleida.

After dithering, as I almost always do when I have to make a decision, I finally opted to change the subject and ask if we might be able to visit the Tower of Panoramas, thereby keeping under wraps the semi-secret goal of my trip, which was in fact to see Cortázar's sealed door and sleep, if at all possible, in that "poky little room" with the closet and clouds and likely views of the solitary pine tree that Bioy had recalled in his parallel story.

The Tower of Panoramas? The tower was still there, he said, but the panoramas not so much. Since by then night was falling over Montevideo, it would be best to leave it until the next day, he added. After that I didn't dare mention that I also wanted to visit the Hotel Cervantes and spend a night in the "poky little room," so Sirés ended up dropping me off, along with the other guests of the Centro Cultural de España, in a hotel very near the Port Market, in the Old Town.

There I met Augusto Nikt, a writer and former whaler, whom I'd never heard of before, which wasn't surprising if you considered that his Polish surname translated as "Nobody." And what was all that about being a former whaler? I was quite sure he'd introduced himself as Nikt, because I'd asked him to spell out his surname, which he did. But one hour later, in bed and ready for sleep, I looked him up online, and not only did I not find any information about him, but I also didn't come across a single other Augusto Nikt, which made me think he must have given me a false name.

He had read Tabucchi in great depth, he said, and wanted to give me his condolences. He had also read plenty of Cortázar. At this, he paused, as if expecting a response. I've read plenty of Cortázar, he repeated. I'm sorry, I said, but why labor the point? I've never labored a point in my life, said Nikt, just as I've never wanted to live in the deserts of the East. Needless to say, this comment threw me somewhat, but I had no chance to delve any deeper into his personality, because shortly afterward, as if annoyed, Augusto Nikt disappeared, and I didn't see him again for the rest of the trip, except once, briefly, when I was leaving Montevideo, and by then, quite frankly, it was too late for everything.

7

By noon the next day, Sirés and I were making our way up to the flat roof of the Tower of Panoramas. At the entrance to the old cenacle, I saw an inscription which I'd already heard about and which someone had fortunately thought to conserve, or restore. The inscription warned, with perfect Herrerian wit: "No Entry to Uruguayans."

But no other traces remained of the glory days. The minuscule physical space from which an entire continent's poetry had been transformed was now an empty, uninspiring room where nothing remained of the decorations that had once adorned the walls, though they could be seen in the pictures that had been kept of the panoramics' salon; those very pictures, which I remembered so well, allowed me to pinpoint the spot on the wall where Mallarmé's photo had been, and that was almost enough for me. Only enough, mind you, not everything, because deep down I had wanted there to be an adjoining room in which time had rewound by a century and where, after getting past the Uruguayans' door policy, I would have found myself instantly enveloped in the great smoky atmosphere of one of those gatherings. After all, it wasn't very difficult to imagine, in that barren, anodyne space, a few poets making crazy attempts to bring new vim and vigor to a language, Spanish, that had been growing stiff and dry, and had basically lost a good deal since its literary Golden Age.

Sirés left the flat roof to climb a spiral staircase to the little viewing platform on top of the empty room, and eventually I resolved to overcome my fear of heights and follow him up. From there, Sirés, who seemed to have recovered his gravelly voice, pointed out various landmarks in the city, among them the glorious and supremely odd Palacio Salvo, an astonishing art deco skyscraper inspired by the *Divine Comedy* and which, if I understood correctly, had stood uninhabited for some time.

I asked if there were any other uninhabited skyscrapers, and Sirés shook his head. The rest of the city, where the French had, at one time, had a considerable presence, was very much inhabited, and the Montevideans, I would soon discover, were on the whole very friendly people, not easily infected by modern hysteria, and inexplicably immune to grumpiness. Some of them smiled in a slow sort of way, as if they had all the time in the world. The houses, the port, the streets, and the beaches all showed signs of a strange, memorable calm, which made the visitor feel he really had arrived in a city where he could live.

This is the place for me, I remember thinking.

And it wasn't such a strange thing to think, because I'd come from Barcelona with its endless tensions, and suddenly I felt I was in a kind of—to put it one way and thinking partly of the Palacio Salvo—Dantean paradise.

Sooner or later, I said to myself, it happens to everyone, if only for a tenth of a second: the paradise drive. And I told Ricardo Sirés about my long-standing relationship with Montevideo and how, many years before, when I was passing through Paris, someone in Barcelona had commissioned me to translate *L'Uruguayen* into Spanish, a book written in French by the Argentinean Raúl Damonte Botana, far better known as Copi, and the only author I've ever translated a book by in my life: a very useful experience for a young man, because at first what was being described seemed so unhinged that I thought I was doing a terrible job of the translation, when really I was just revealing the book's true imaginative force and the capacity of any story to go beyond all reasonable bounds. In other words, as I translated *L'Uruguayen,* my writing peered for the first time into the abyss of the most unfettered panoramas.

"They have words for everything here. There's one for saying, 'This is the place for me,' and it's the very name of the city: Montevideo," Copi had written in *L'Uruguayen.* And that phrase, "This is the place for me," had stayed with me ever since, and I found, that day on the tower's flat roof, the ideal spot from which to think it again, until I saw that recovering it in practice meant repeating to myself the word I found most moving at that moment: *Montevideo.*

"Montevideo, a city that sounds like a verse," I remembered Borges had written. And incidentally, as I was telling him about *L'Uruguayen,* Ricardo Sirés had stubbornly remained on the little viewing platform above the empty room, even after I'd climbed back down in order to feel closer to that timeworn flat roof, and I couldn't fathom what Sirés found so appealing about that viewing platform until I realized that it was simply the more extensive panorama.

Come back up, Sirés was saying. He wanted to tell me how appalled Herrera y Reissig would have been to see how the view had changed. Because even the Mar de la Plata, he said, must look different now. Come back up, he said again. No, I replied, this is the place for me. And in the end I emerged victorious from that absurd stand-off, and Sirés, wild-haired from the wind, was forced to abandon his panoramas and climb back down the spiral staircase for good. What shall we do now? he asked. If you like, I said, I'll recount a battle between the Greeks and the Trojans, any one you like. And as we laughed, I had a sense that the panoramas were resigning themselves to a discreet background role while the tower enjoyed the limelight that the years had so unjustly taken from it.

8

We were strolling through the Old Town when I decided the time had finally come to ask about the Cervantes Hotel, since I was, I said, extremely curious about it. Sirés froze right there in the middle of the street. He seemed genuinely surprised. The Cervantes? he asked, then calm returned to his face. From a radio inside a house there came the sound of the "Bolero sonámbulo," performed by Ry Cooder and Manuel Galbán. It's called the Esplendor these days, Sirés said at last. It's a boutique hotel in the Barrio de las Artes, and I think it's also been turned into a cultural center. I explained I was keen to see a very particular room, and spend a night there if possible. Sirés got the wrong end of the stick and thought I was unhappy with the hotel arranged for me by the Centro Cultural de España, and I had to explain that I had no problem whatsoever with the accommodation they'd provided, and simply wanted to look into a very particular detail in one of the rooms at the Esplendor. I went on to explain my reason for wanting to spend a night in that hotel, which we immediately began heading toward. The whole way there, still keeping quiet about my writer's block—I didn't want him to see me as a wretched victim of my best-known book—I talked nonstop, first about the hectic life I led in Barcelona and how much writing I was getting done—total lies, but gripping nonetheless—and then, a few steps from the Esplendor (the Resplandor, I called it), we agreed that, once inside, we'd ask which room contained the sealed door hidden by a closet that I was so keen to inspect.

In the lobby of the Esplendor, which had changed a great deal since the description in "The Sealed Door," the receptionist, whom I immediately began calling the "manager," directly influenced by Cortázar's story, was taken aback by my request for such a specific room. And he also seemed very surprised, too surprised, that Cortázar had once been a guest in that establishment. Gardel had been, he said; Gardel had sung in the old Cervantes and even spent the night. And Borges, Norah Lange, José Luis Romero, and Atahualpa Yupanqui had stayed there as well, but as for Cortázar . . . .

He was surprised, but soon pulled himself together, saying that since the Esplendor was not only a hotel but also a newly opened cultural center, he would be only too pleased to do his duty and look into it for us. It's a matter of great interest, I said. Yes, of course, said the mustached manager, it's quite something, Cortázar staying here, plus it could really bring in the Japanese tourists.

I was perplexed to hear him mention Asian tourists instead of, say, Argentinean tourists, and Sirés confirmed the absurdity of that link between Cortázar and the Japanese, a connection he'd never heard anyone else make, meaning that most likely, he said, the manager was pulling our leg.

As if the manager weren't enough, he was suddenly joined by his assistant, a chatty underling hell-bent on showing us the parking lot beneath the hotel, where, he told us, the stage and stalls and even the balconies and ticket booths of what had once been the Cervantes Theater, and subsequently cinema, could still be found, all in mint condition and soon to be listed as "cultural heritage," though now functioning as a parking lot.

What we saw in that ghostly basement was a curious blend of garage and theater, parking lot and cinema; a somewhat claustrophobic space packed full of all kinds of vehicles, and if there was one thing I found monumentally boring it was cars, motorbikes, repair shops, diesel engines, wheels, and tires. Even a few ticket booths could make me lose the will to live if they happened to be in a garage. And there in the basement of the Esplendor, the ticket booths were exactly as they had been—I imagined—when the whole of Montevideo had gathered there to listen to Carlos Gardel.

Our immersion in that underground world was the most tedious thing I'd experienced in a long time. Eventually, the ghostly vehicular overload got the better of my patience and, unable to stand any more walking around that soon-to-be site of cultural heritage, I pretended that I felt a strange, stifling darkness all around me and, feigning a choking fit (I conjured up an implausible allergy to gasoline stored in basements), convinced them to return us safe and sound to the reception, where the manager looked rather put out to see us again, as if annoyed that we'd escaped from the dungeons of his castle, and asked if we hadn't liked "the famous basement."

9

Surely, I said to the manager, someone in the hotel must know the number of the second-floor room where Cortázar's story takes place. And I asked again if I could take that room for a single night. For a moment I thought they were going to send us back to the garage. The minutes went by, and there seemed to be no possibility whatsoever of identifying the room. And meanwhile, standing in the reception, Sirés and I were being steadily surrounded by hotel staff and guests, though none of them seemed to have heard of the sealed door.

Eventually, someone who worked at the hotel—in various capacities, he clarified—came to our aid, and this made all the difference. He was a young man with the "deep, booming voice of Uruguayans" that Cortázar describes in his story, and he said his name was Nicomedes and then described himself as an "all-terrain vehicle," since he worked on both the admin side of things and cleaning the rooms. Precisely thanks to the latter, he knew there was only one room in the hotel with a door to an adjoining room that was covered by a closet. It has to be on the second floor, I said. And Nicomedes, smiling, confirmed that it was.

Next, using Cortázar's story as a guide, I asked him if the second floor was still a vast space with "Petrone's door and that of the lone woman" at one end, and if, between the two doors, there was still that "plinth supporting an appalling replica of the Venus de Milo."

No Venus, the manager interrupted, she was taken away years ago. And Nicomedes nodded in agreement, though when he tried to talk about the warehouse where that "appalling replica" had ended up, the manager stopped him, as if annoyed at him for giving away information that I had no reason to know. And yet, two minutes later, that same manager was revealing the number of the room I was looking for. It's Room 205, he said, but someone's currently in there. It'll be available in an hour or two.

Next to the manager, his assistant, and Nicomedes, another member of hotel staff, with an equally deep, booming voice, was at that moment telling a guest the story of his friend Rodolfo, who one day simply stopped washing, shaving, and getting out of bed, and eventually stopped speaking and died. It was odd, because the fact that he'd died didn't shock me as much as the fact that he'd stopped speaking, as if I had a strange affinity with any sort of silence that wasn't related to death.

Then all of a sudden the guest, who had no doubt heard—and with obvious interest—what we'd been saying about the sealed door, expressed his amazement that we could still remember a writer who'd been dead for so many years. But it's Cortázar, so it's hardly strange we're talking about him, said Nicomedes, letting slip that he wasn't completely indifferent to the creator of cronopios. Yes, said the guest—who handed Sirés and me a card showing that his name was Ochs and he was a maker of dolls—but it's not easy for writers, believe me, even the greatest ones, to pull off the miracle of the encore, the beautiful being-again.

This caused a kind of verbal short-circuit, and something like a general sense that it would be impossible to say anything more extraordinarily cheesy about the resurrection of a writer who, what's more, had never been dismissed or forgotten.

Look at us, I said to the guest. None of us wants to "be again."

To be again, *that is the question,* Sirés joked, trying to calm everyone down and move on from this unforeseen mix-up caused by our search for a number, 205. But things went from bad to worse when the manager tried to join in the party, again flaunting his special talent for saying the first thing that came into his head. Deep down, he explained in as many words, you write to be remembered, to win the internal battle against amnesia, against the gray hole of time, to surrender to the page as a pharaoh's mummy surrenders to the bandages and ointments, I don't know any better way than that of achieving the miracle of the encore.

He looked so pleased with what he'd just said that I took the unnecessary risk of telling him no one would ever swallow that business of the "gray hole of time," let alone the "miracle of the encore." And then, not content with telling him that, I added that there was something Argentinean about him. And, well, let's just say that I would never wish for anyone to be looked at the way the manager looked at me then. I think if I'd gone on to say that sometimes, because of his physique, he reminded me of Mini Mustache, i.e., Hitler, and at other times of Big Mustache, i.e., Stalin, by now I would be Dead Mustache.

I can't say I was happy with how things were going, because for years I'd wanted to come face-to-face with that door behind the closet, for years I'd hoped to one day enter that room and stand in "the exact place where the fantastical bursts into Cortázar's story," and now, mere minutes and mere yards away from that door and that old closet, I had made a terrible blunder.

And Sirés couldn't help me out, because he was horrified by what I'd done. Nicomedes, on the other hand, did come to my aid, showing that he was somehow on my side and, moreover, that of all the people in that huge crowd milling around us, summoned by the sound of Cortázar's name, he was the only one who had actually read the Argentinean writer.

"Drenched in bees," Nicomedes announced, and then seemed not to remember the rest of what he was going to say, or perhaps he did remember it and had simply been aiming to confuse the situation further. But to what end?

"Drenched in bees" could also have been a password, or a watchword beyond my comprehension, but in the end it turned out to be no more than the beginning of a poem by Cortázar that Nicomedes knew and that, eventually, after going to his office and finding the rest of it, he returned to the reception to read to us: "Drenched in bees, [. . .] and amid smiling enemies my hands weave the legend."

I thought Nicomedes might have been subtly letting me know that this whole agglomeration of hotel staff, who seemed like the manager's praetorian guard, were my "smiling enemies"—that he was trying to warn me in front of the manager himself.

I looked around, and sure enough, the sowers of confusion, who in that reception gave the impression of having challenged me and emerged victorious, were smiling, especially the maker of dolls, Señor Ochs, who I noticed was the one who most resembled a queen bee.

"Ochs," I said to him, "do bees seem real to you?"

I think I asked that simply for the chance to pronounce the name Ochs. After all, it was a completely gratuitous question, devoid of all purpose or meaning, though it might yet have acquired purpose and meaning with the doll maker's response; everything depended on him, on that cheesy proponent of "being-again."

"All I know," he said, "is that a half-truth is a total lie."

10

We agreed that Sirés and I would go for a walk around the city, and then, as soon as Room 205 was empty, in two or three hours' time, they'd let us know via WhatsApp. They could hardly be trusted, not least after our locking of horns, and yet we had no choice but to wait for Manager Mustache to do us a favor, or for Señor Ochs to hear a whole truth.

We left behind that cabin full of Marx brothers and set out to get some fresh air. And the first thing we did was make for Calle Camacuá opposite La Brecha, where the highly mysterious Comte de Lautréamont had lived, a man who gave up Montevideo for France at the age of fourteen and whom I now greeted in my head as if he were my oldest, dearest friend. And indeed, I'd been fifteen when I read his *Chants de Maldoror,* and they were a huge revelation to me. But searching Montevideo for traces of the count was never an easy task, particularly since, as Sirés said, the city had a habit of keeping its past hidden behind the most unbelievable advertising billboards, for example on Avenida 18 de Julio, where almost none of the exceptional art nouveau architecture was visible to passersby.

We walked down Calle Camacuá toward somewhere rather more prosaic, the offices of the Centro Cultural de España, where I met Sirés's charming colleagues. A great atmosphere. And I also called in on a class in the writing school they'd set up there, to answer some of the students' questions. One of them wanted to know if I wrote on a computer, and I explained that I wrote with a fountain pen, always by hand, at which point an older lady came out with the question of the day, asking what color ink I put in my pen. Normally black, I said, but then I edit in red and give the pages to Romina, my secretary, to make a hat with.

When Sirés and I resumed our stroll around the city, I distinctly remember passing in front of the Solís Theater. There, Sirés paused to explain that it was the oldest theater in the world, before quickly backtracking to clarify that really it was only the oldest in Latin America, which to be honest came as quite a relief, since I wasn't sure how I ought to react to the sudden sight, halfway through a walk around Montevideo, of the oldest theater in the world. I thought of Mario Gas, a friend from my younger days and fellow law student. I'd always heard it said that Mario, a thespian to the core, had been born right here in Montevideo, when his parents, great actors, were touring Latin America. And it occurred to me that in the forties, when Mario was born, his parents must have been working in a Montevideo theater of a similar stripe to the Solís.

After the walk, itself boasting some magnificent moments, such as when we strolled along the imposing Río de la Plata and I spoke to Sirés of Alexandre Dumas and the Trojan War, inventing a fair amount, because I knew next to nothing about Dumas, we ended up going into a restaurant near the Plaza Independencia, worn out and ravenously hungry. We were already on our desserts, enjoying an exceptional chajá cake, when Sirés received—we thought the moment would never come—a WhatsApp message from the Esplendor, saying that the room was now available. This cheered me up no end, because it meant I'd have ample time to examine something which, thinking about it, and as had already occurred to the more pragmatic Sirés, would really perhaps require only a quick, keen-eyed look: a glance at once swift and penetrating that would instantly reveal the form, if indeed it had a form, of the meeting point between real life and fiction, which lay hidden right there in Montevideo, behind that old closet.

11

That meeting point between real life and fiction was taking up more and more space in my mind, perhaps because I felt I was on the threshold of what would most likely be a unique experience, though I didn't rule out the opposite possibility. Still, I preferred to think the former was what I had in store.

At any rate, that afternoon I went into the room with the sealed door, and at first nothing out of the ordinary seemed to result from my having entered that place, in other words, my having entered the very setting of the story.

I did, however, experience the sensation described by

Andrés Di Tella in his *Notebooks:* "The Paris boulevards in Godard's *Une femme mariée* and the Monument Valley plains in John Ford's *My Darling Clementine,* all in the same unsparing black and white, were like neighborhoods in the same city. The images brought on *the desire to go in search of those places,* but, at the same time, the suspicion that those locations couldn't exist."

That was how I felt, but then I told myself that I hadn't crossed the Atlantic in search of the sealed door only to enter that room and find it seemed like a place that couldn't possibly exist and yet at the same time existed. No. That room existed. I was in it, I'd just stepped into it. It was a solid, obvious fact. I was moving around a real place, although if anyone had seen me at that moment I might not have seemed so real to them, wandering around and gazing at reality in total astonishment, as if I'd never encountered it before in my life. You see, everything was precisely identical to the way Cortázar had described that room in his story.

Was I in the story? Was that how it felt? Well, I said to myself, I'm in the room.

And it was touching to see how for the sink, for example, no time had passed. The bathroom window was indeed larger than the window in the room itself, and looked mournfully out onto a wall and a distant, almost pointless patch of sky. For a long while I stared, almost hypnotized, at that "pointless patch of sky" and its clouds, and while I was at it I looked for and found the lone tree in the street, the pine that stood on the same block as the hotel and had been described by Bioy in his parallel story to Cortázar's. And I was surprised to see a man, in a building very close to that pine tree, sliding a plank of wood out of his window and into the window of another apartment building.

With the exception of what was behind the closet, I examined the room so thoroughly that once or twice I got lost in unexpected nooks and crannies, down paths I'd never before taken and which led me to the Montevideo of Onetti and then to the Madrid of that same Onetti, whom I once saw sitting on his indestructible bed, with a bottle of whiskey and some glasses by his side, and a door and a closet behind him, refusing to be filmed by my friends, until eventually he relented and said to the camera a phrase so charmingly humane that I incorporated it into my lexicon forevermore:

"Have it your way, but only because I'm nice."

12

Lost in my detailed study of that day's sky, I realized I hadn't even noticed something that in normal circumstances would never have escaped my attention: although the room had been thoroughly cleaned, smelled of roses throughout, and was impeccably, almost geometrically tidy, there was one anomaly: between the closet and the window, someone had left behind a rather old-fashioned red suitcase, a suitcase from another age, in pretty good condition.

Could it have belonged to the previous guest? Nothing of the sort had ever happened to me before, but it seemed plausible. I was about to call down and ask Sirés, who was waiting in the lobby, to come and tell me what he thought I should do with this suitcase that had inveigled its way into my life and into Cortázar's story and, what was more, weighed several pounds. But in the end I opted to take it into the corridor myself, as if I couldn't allow that offending object to remain there, on my territory, for a second longer. After leaving the suitcase outside, I called the manager on the hotel phone to ask if someone could come and collect it. And the manager, as if it were quite normal for there to be a suitcase belonging to the previous guest in my room, simply told me that he'd send someone—and here he took a very deep breath, as if he were about to pass out from overwork—when he got the chance.

Barely a moment later, I heard footsteps in the corridor and opened the door, naively thinking someone had come right away to collect the suitcase. However, I was surprised to find that the footsteps belonged, not to a member of hotel staff, but rather to a guest in a trench coat who was visibly drunk and stopped right in front of me to say, before I'd even opened my mouth, that he knew full well his coat made him look like a wealthy man but in fact he was destitute.

Still, what a nerve to show up here so drunk, was the most I dared to say, and even that seemed rather bold, given I didn't know him at all. I'd told him off, but in a playful tone, which he'd surely picked up on. Now listen to me, said the man, if you're one of those people who think this world is bad, you ought to see some of the others.

The others? I was about to respond that I knew them all like the back of my hand, because I, like every person I'd ever laid eyes on in my life, was an imaginary being, but I stopped myself because that penniless drunkard wouldn't have understood a word I'd said if I ventured into that murky terrain and opened his eyes to the broadly fictitious nature of our existence.

I went straight back into my room—I already considered it my room by then, and all the more so for having banished the red suitcase—and took a first look at the closet, which seemed older than it had a few minutes before. I opened it and inside was an odd collection of useless objects, including a thimble and several reels of different-colored thread. I remembered my mother's response when I told her that I was leaving for Paris because Barcelona was insufferable and Franco was a criminal. You'll have to mend your own clothes over there, she told me, and if by any chance you decide to go to Russia, they'll put you to work and make you sweat like a pig.

I shut the closet and decided to leave the inspection of the sealed door until my return; it deserved its own special session, when I could give it my full attention and calmly scrutinize all there was to see there, assuming, that is, there was anything to see. So I went down to the lobby and rejoined Sirés, who said, without a hint of anger in his voice, that he'd been waiting too long, and to whom I decided not to mention either the red suitcase or the blind-drunk man who'd told me he was destitute. I wanted to preempt what I suspected Sirés would tell me: that what with that suitcase and the drunken guest, someone had served me the beginning of a story on a plate and I'd surely end up writing it. The thing is, I didn't want it to be Sirés who pushed me to start writing again. I thought I'd rather decide for myself to return to it, which, knowing how indecisive I was and despite the fact that I sometimes—rarely—didn't feel dead set against it, might not be for a while yet: it would depend, I thought, on me spotting a chance to change my style, something that was bound to happen sooner or later. After all, it's well known that an author is no more than the transformations of their style, and it was only logical for that to be true for me as well.

Besides, Sirés seemed to be a *recommender* at heart. All through lunch he hadn't stopped recommending me books—by Simenon and Eduardo Galeano; movies—everything by John Ford; famous websites and blogs; plays—Chekhov and Plautus; and songs, including all of Françoise Hardy, all of Jacques Dutronc, and "Caballo viejo," performed by Simón Díaz.

Nothing I didn't already know, aside from the Díaz cover. What was more, when he ventured to make recommendations relating to a person's private life, he always churned out the most hackneyed of phrases, which is something I find deeply infuriating; the sorts of phrases that are so neat as to be practically soulless and that even have something of the spirit of a box-office girl from another age, of those women with so much professionalism and so many hands for dispensing tickets but not one eye, not one remotely original gaze that could form an opinion on what they were selling.

Was Sirés a potential box-office girl? I pondered this question throughout our lunch, to keep my mind occupied and avoid the temptation to tell him about the disturbing—or perhaps simply strange—matter of the red suitcase I had found in my room.

Possibly sensing that I was hiding something, he asked what I was thinking about. Oh, nothing, nothing, I replied. Or rather, I went on, I was thinking about how much I'd like—I tried to frighten him—to meddle in other people's lives, to reshape the moral existence of everyone I've met in Montevideo. Sirés looked at me in surprise and then burst out laughing. For example, I carried on, undaunted, I'd like to spend my time uniting or separating people from themselves and their lovers. Since it's so long since I've written anything—and on saying this, I realized with some horror that I had now confessed my tragic writer's block and there was no going back—I could at least write *in life itself*, in the real world, achieving divorces and tears and forging marriages, boycotting bourgeois peace, do you see what I mean?

This is news to me, he said. I didn't know you'd gone so long without writing, but anyway, we can discuss it all tomorrow when I interview you on stage. You can talk then about how much you love interfering in other people's relationships, reshaping their moral existence, and there's nothing wrong, by the way, with devoting yourself to that, body and soul; I wouldn't mind giving it a try myself. I didn't want to tell him that he'd been trying it all along with his tawdry recommendations. Well, said Sirés, let's see what happens tomorrow, although, come to think of it, attempting to make some couple in the audience get divorced might complicate matters a little too much, especially for me, since I'm the one who has to stay here in Montevideo.

"I understand completely," I said. "Have it your way, but only because I'm nice."

13

For the rest of the day we rehearsed in the auditorium, the Estela Medina Hall, located in the basement of the Centro Cultural de España. We went over the long interview that would take place late the following afternoon—and in fact the timing would be a bit tight, because my flight was leaving shortly before midnight—in front of an underground audience.

Eventually we agreed not to go into the business of *writ-*

ing in real life, indeed to avoid it altogether. And we also decided not so much as to mention *Virtuosos of Suspense* and instead to focus on Cortázar's Montevideo story, using it as an example of the kinds of stories that belong to narrative trend number three from my list, stories that organize themselves around the very obstacle (in this case, an old door behind a closet) that prevents us from being told the full story while still allowing the reader to travel a long way.

I suggested quoting Miles Davis's question to Mallarmé: "Aren't you writing the very thing that hinders your writing?" But Sirés convinced me that it wouldn't be appropriate— neither the fake story about Davis and Mallarmé nor the suggestion that I'd always set out to write the very thing that hindered my writing, when really I'd just gone a long time without doing any work.

"Isn't that right?" he asked.

Sirés had me exhausted; I'd even say, as per the song, old and tired. What's more, his general run-through of what we were going to do the next day in the Estela Medina seemed completely pointless to me: in the end, its sole purpose had been to establish what we *weren't* going to talk about. And I was so shattered that evening when I got back to Room 205 that for a few seconds all I could think about was crawling into bed and trying to rest as much as possible and putting off, until I was feeling better, the inspection of that tantalizing exact place behind the closet where the fantastical had burst into Cortázar's story.

Moving the closet proved surprisingly easy. It was so old and fragile that I was more worried about accidentally breaking it and having it fall to pieces on top of me.

Once I'd carefully maneuvered it out of the way, half of

the sealed door was revealed. And it turned out to be ajar, which needless to say was quite a shock, because it seemed like an invitation to go into the next room. I poked my head around the door to see what could be glimpsed of that place I never thought I'd see, in which, according to Cortázar, a solitary woman had consoled a crying child. I didn't expect, of course, to see the woman, but nor did I expect to see nothing at all, and as it happened, I was faced with the deepest darkness I'd encountered in my life.

Did I have to go in if the room was in darkness? And at the same time, what was I expecting to find in there? A sudden revelation? An epiphany, in the form of a vision, would have been ideal—I'd always been fascinated by what Beckett said on the jetty looking out to sea at Killiney Bay: "At the end of the jetty, in the howling wind, never to be forgotten, when suddenly I saw the whole thing. The vision, at last."

I envied the vision I knew Beckett had had: that the darkness, which he'd worked so hard to fend off, was in fact his best ally, because only within it would he be able to make out the world he had to create in order to breathe.

The darkness of Room 206 would have filled me with awe and even fear had I not remembered the darkness Beckett had chosen on the jetty, although I decided it would be better to wait for daylight before stepping into the room. So I left it all as I'd found it: the door to Room 206 ajar and the closet covering it once more, providing a handy barricade. But as I turned away from the closet, I had the feeling someone was staring at the back of my neck. I didn't look around, because there couldn't possibly be anyone behind me, and also because the energy felt so intense that I was afraid there really *was* someone there. Good thing I covered the half-open door back up, I thought. But when I sat down on my bed, I heard an object fall in the darkened room, an object that was obviously tiny and that rolled, for three interminable seconds, along the floor. I wouldn't sleep easily if there was anyone in there. Or indeed if there wasn't.

14

But I soon dozed off, without hearing any more ominous sounds. I found myself remembering a demented soldier I'd met in the Melilla military asylum, a madman who used to kneel, laughing, in front of an anthill, and who had somehow taken on the role of a kind of Fortune or Destiny figure for the ants, sometimes trying to drive them crazy and sometimes to calm them down and make them fall back in line, all with the help of a simple pine cone.

After the madman with the ants, I moved on to the Argentinean writer Néstor Sánchez, the very person responsible for my discovering Cortázar. Or rather, I would have taken longer to arrive at Cortázar had I not encountered, in the Áncora y Delfín bookshop in Barcelona, a copy of *Us Two,* one of the first novels by Néstor Sánchez, who would be the only writer I tried to imitate when I wrote *Nepal.*

Néstor Sánchez, that secret Cortázar. I knew he'd taken his own escape from Argentina so far that some followers thought he was dead and held an homage to him in Buenos Aires. When, to everyone's surprise, they heard he was alive and well and had just returned to the city after years spent traveling the world on bizarre adventures, they went to see him, to demand that he tell them why the hell he'd gone so long without writing.

"Well, my epic came to an end," was his laconic reply.

I woke up in the middle of the night, just as I was most thoroughly embroiled in a hypothetical set of Russian dolls with Néstor Sánchez as the secret figure, the tall shadow crouching within Julio Cortázar. I was awoken by a furious knocking at my door. When I realized it had to be part of the real world and not the dream, I felt terrified by that concerted effort to invade my room. But even amid the distress of such a violent awakening, I had time to notice that the sealed door, perhaps because it was hidden by the closet once more, gave off nothing but pure calm, total peace, and immense serenity, while the only door into the room from the corridor was being practically flattened by this woman beating it with her fists and shouting to be let in. Why did no one at the glorious reception desk react, when that hotel amplified every sound?

15

Those were testing moments for me, listening to that woman who was speaking, or rather jabbering, sentences in English. I put two and two together and deduced that she must be the owner of the red suitcase. I got out of bed and went to the door, pressed my ear against it, and heard, on the other side, the ragged breath of this would-be caller, a woman who was evidently very annoyed and seemed capable of anything. I decided not to open the door, since I didn't know what I might find, and instead suggested to the woman that she ask in reception for her suitcase. But all she did, on hearing this advice delivered in Spanish, was rattle the door even harder and start shouting in that language instead.

"Make them stop, make those idiots pack it in, make them stop reproducing once and for all!"

Who was she talking about?

Humanity as a whole, it seemed.

My terror increased when I realized this fragile door was all that separated me from a person who wanted to do away with everything once and for all, or perhaps only the filthy steaming hordes who crowd the streets and who she perhaps thought were located in this very room with its rickety closet and secret half-open door, which compared with the main door was a veritable oasis of calm, where fiction and reality seemed to be curled up together, at peace.

And that peace allowed me to take myself in hand and let the furious woman's raging subside. Which it did. And when I heard her walking away down the corridor, I breathed a sigh of relief. Left behind like a dream was what had never been. I wanted to believe—really, just so as not to go mad—that the woman had argued with her lover in that same room the morning before and then stormed out, slamming the door and leaving him there in bed. And perhaps this man, when his lover seemed to be taking a long time to return, had vacated the room at check-out time and left the red suitcase right where it was.

But that was just one of many possible explanations. I've always wondered what might have happened if I'd opened the door. Most likely, nothing particularly exciting. Because she was hoping to vent her rage on someone else, in all likelihood she would have been so disappointed on seeing me that I would have become the true victim of the misunderstanding.

At any rate, I'll never know what might have happened. The minutes went by and she didn't return. And just as I was thinking that whoever in the hotel had taken her suitcase must have given it back—I had begun to call these people "the suspects," because they seemed to form part of a vague League of Suspected Conspirators of the Reception Desk—I discovered that the woman was still shouting, albeit now a long way from my room; she seemed to have relocated her tantrum to the first floor, or perhaps she was in reception.

Make them stop, make them pack it in, I heard her say again. And the whole hotel was like an echo chamber—not surprising, considering that in these corridors even the slightest sound was deafening. But after a few minutes, when I least expected it, the red-suitcase lady's racket stopped. Feeling so liberated by this promising new development, I cast around for a way to celebrate, and although it was possible that hearing a noise on the second floor might bring the woman back, I decided to take my chances and, without even waiting for the first light of day, went ahead and moved the closet again, this time rather more stealthily, to reveal the sealed door for a second time.

16

It was possible to reach the other side. That's what happens when a wall is a wall and a door at the same time. Perhaps at that moment the circumstances were conspiring to allow that to take place. As Geneste, the archaeologist from Herzog's documentary, has said, walls can talk to us, accept or reject us.

On this occasion, both wall and half-open door accepted me. Although that dense darkness was still there, I overcame my fear and took a few steps—again, as you'd expect, without seeing a thing. And now I was in. But my God, why hadn't I waited until I'd had a proper breakfast the next morning before going into that room? I paused and went no farther, just stared at the darkness for a good long while. I stared as if this were the darkness enveloping the jetty that looked out to sea at the port of Killiney, as if it had human eyes. And I found the courage to wait for the darkness to grow gradually less black. When that began to happen, I could still see little enough to assume the room was completely empty, with no furniture or anything else. But I was wrong. In the very center of that deserted space, there stood a red suitcase. The suitcase of the moment, the trusty summer suitcase, the suitcase of that crazy shouting lady on the landing. The red suitcase, the suitcase we drag along a jetty in the rain, only without the vision.

Had "the suspects" put it there? Why hadn't they given it back to the door-basher? That question helped me to see more clearly. The shadows slowly dispersed, and I made out a hefty black shape resting on the handle of the suitcase, a shape that soon revealed itself to be a giant spider, some six inches wide, and dead, dead as a doornail.

Solid, huge, repugnant, and in no way artificial like the one in Cascais, that spider came as such a shock that I took a step back, as if to follow some advice I was once given by Madeleine Moore: you'll soon realize that the most important thing is not dying for ideas, styles, or theories but rather taking a step back and maintaining a distance between ourselves and the things that happen to us.

The moment I distanced myself from what I'd just seen, I realized that was the end of my incursion into the next room, into the unpleasant realm of that monstrous arthropod that had four pairs of legs and was dead, stone dead, on top of a suitcase in a space where a sad baby had once cried and been tenderly consoled by its solitary mother.

17

I'd only gone there to see what happened when a person set eyes on "the exact place where the fantastical bursts into Cortázar's story," but everything had become very complicated and I'd taken it too far, because I couldn't imagine Petrone from "The Sealed Door" physically entering the adjoining room.

I went back to bed, leaving the sealed door ajar, precisely as I'd found it, but replacing the closet just in case. And in that bed once again, restless and lost, I waited for dawn so I could be the first person to go down to breakfast, and then later inspect the adjoining room with more light and fewer setbacks, perhaps even finding out what the object was that I'd heard fall to the floor the previous night.

Since I'd brought with me Juan Eduardo Cirlot's *Dictionary of Symbols,* which I'd been meaning to read for years and had only flicked through absent-mindedly between moments of indecision on the flight, I decided the time had finally come to explore it, and the first thing I looked up was the entry for "door."

As you'd expect, Cirlot's words on the matter were essential reading: "Doors are thresholds, crossings, but they also seem linked to the idea of home, homeland, worlds that we abandon and to which we return, always by passing through doors. The door is a feminine symbol in the sense of an opening, an invitation to penetrate mysteries; the opposite of a wall, which would represent the masculine."

That "invitation to penetrate mysteries," I thought, was very much a characteristic of the sealed door. And I returned to Cirlot's entry for "door" to discover that, almost begrudgingly, as if it were just a way of concluding that entry in the *Dictionary,* Cirlot had slipped in a very brief Nordic historical anecdote, which for its power alone seemed to demand a separate space in the same book, as well as providing me—a by no means insignificant detail—with a magnificent opportunity to travel a very long way.

Reykjavík

In ancient Scandinavia, Juan Eduardo Cirlot tells us, exiles took the doors to their houses with them when they left or, in other cases, threw them overboard into the sea and then disembarked in the place where the doors made landfall, seeing it as a sign that the hand of fate had deliberately led them there. It's said that this is how Reykjavík, the capital of Iceland, was founded, in the year 874.

Bogotá

1

Doors, Cirlot said, are an invitation to penetrate mysteries—the opposite of walls, which represent the masculine.
His words couldn't have been more applicable to my relationship thus far with "The Sealed Door." And I could also,
of course, have applied them to myself, as I wrestled with a
thousand different dilemmas before going down to breakfast. One of these was whether, since it was now getting
light, I should delay the café con leche awaiting me at breakfast and dare to take a closer look at the room next door.
But the thought of another encounter with that repugnant
spectacle kept holding me back. And so I decided to put off
my inspection of Room 206, at the same time telling myself
that it would be very lazy not to one day set down in writing
some of what was happening to me, which at times was very
strange indeed.

I propped myself up on my elbows and got out of bed,
ready to go and have breakfast, thinking I'd inspect the adjoining room on my return. I dressed quickly and stepped
out onto the landing—in too much of a hurry to notice that
the door to Room 206, and indeed the room itself, had vanished—and made my way down those stairs that had creaked
so conspicuously for decades, wondering all the while when

enormous spiders had started choosing the handles of red suitcases for their home and tomb.

Once in the breakfast room, which doubled as a bar in the evenings, I ordered fried eggs with bacon, a café con leche, and some Uruguayan alfajores. The television was on and I recognized the movie that was showing, *Tropic Moon,* based on a Simenon novel. "In the night, after I blew out the candle," one character was saying, "I could still see, despite the darkness, the pale cage of the mosquito net, and beyond it a vast empty space where scorpions, mosquitoes, and spiders seemed to be moving around."

I couldn't help thinking of myself the previous night, lying in bed and trying to make out the sounds, the tremors in the air, and to identify the sudden silences. While I was finishing my breakfast, Nicomedes came over and asked, almost brusquely:

"What's the latest from over there?"

"Over there?"

That's it, I thought. Once again I'm faced with another true fiction; it's like I attract them. Maybe they're figments of my imagination, but all the same, it's not normal for Nicomedes to be talking to me as if he'd known me all his life, or as if he wanted to know me for the rest of it.

By *over there,* Nicomedes meant the Barcelona in which I lived and where, according to him, there existed a certain kind of European intellectual who, as Cortázar said in *Hopscotch,* was convinced that somewhere in Paris there was a key and went hunting for it like a madman.

"Note that I say 'like a madman,' since in fact these people had no idea they were searching for the key, or that the key even existed," said Nicomedes, before clarifying that what he'd just said was also taken from *Hopscotch.*

I saw that he was looking at me as if I didn't believe him, when really it was more that I wasn't very familiar with *Hopscotch*. I had a dog-eared copy at home, but only because a friend from Lugo had turned up at my house with it, devoured the whole thing, and then left it behind on my shelf. But in fact I'd only ever read a few pages, and deep down I had a kind of phobia of the book. I hated it because in the seventies it was much admired by young people my age who wanted to belong to a generation, something that always left me cold. And in fact, I thought, if I had to belong to a generation, I'd rather be an exiled American and, moreover, from another time, a writer from the 1920s, "lost generation" style.

I'd read some of Cortázar's stories—the most famous, the most acclaimed. Perhaps because it was often said in those days that his stories were better than his novels, something I thought I could confirm without having read *Hopscotch*. Or a great deal else. I wasn't a Cortázar fan, but nor was I a detractor. My knowledge of his work didn't go beyond a few vague notions about his writing, really a few clichés about his imagination and his sometimes avant-garde provocations, such as the novel *62: A Model Kit,* which was profoundly influenced by the spirit of the May Revolution in Paris and which I always gave up on at page 68.

But Nicomedes still didn't believe that I believed him, and therefore clarified further, in his deep, booming Uruguayan voice:

"Chapter Twenty-Six."

He seemed to be waiting for me to say something of interest to his conspiratorial side, being as he was a suspected member of the League of Suspected Conspirators. But I couldn't help seeing "Chapter Twenty-Six" as a password, so I tried to think about what might follow and hazarded a guess, despite knowing full well that I could easily end up sounding ridiculous.

"Spider," I said.

Stunned silence.

"Fat and hairy, dead," I added.

It was worth a shot. But I was just making a fool of myself. And worst of all, I could see the horror on Nicomedes's face. This was then replaced by a broad smile, perhaps to mask it. By now I'd made such a total, utter fool of myself that I thought continuing to do so for a little longer wouldn't do any harm, but in the end the frozen expression of astonishment on Nicomedes's face put me off. He must have thought it was a word association game I'd just made up, which was perhaps why he responded, deadpan:

"Tacuarembó."

At that, not having the slightest idea what he was getting at, I entered the realm of wild speculations. Speculations that Nicomedes interrupted by saying, presumably in an effort to be politer to me, that he'd been up late the night before playing poker, and one of the players, a trainee notary, had been ruined, or rather, had lost what little he had.

I decided I'd had enough breakfast and opted to wash my hands of Nicomedes's friendly but cryptic chat and go back to my room, though not without first winding him up a little by saying that I hadn't realized they had notaries in Montevideo as well. Most of the notaries in Uruguay are from this city, he replied. Whatever you say, I said. And I set off toward my room. As I climbed the cacophonous stairs, I wondered once more if I ought to examine the adjoining room by the light of day. By then I was keen to return to Barcelona. I was missing my office and my isolated bedroom, with its TV facing the bed and total absence of adjoining rooms. And it occurred to me that Cirlot had it exactly right when he said that doors were thresholds, crossings, but that they also seemed linked to the idea of home and homeland, worlds we leave behind in order to return to them later.

2

It was on reaching the second floor that I had the deeply disturbing realization—at first I thought I'd gone to the wrong landing—that Room 206 had quite literally disappeared. Without a trace. I could have gotten muddled up with the numbers on the doors the day before or even that very morning, but one thing was undeniable: in the place where the door to Room 206 should have been, the door to that dilapidated room where I'd spied the suitcase and gigantic spider, there was nothing but a white wall.

I hurried into my own room, thinking I could reach number 206 via the sealed door instead. I wasn't going to stand by and let them send me mad. But when I moved the closet just enough to get past, I found that the door to the adjoining room was now unusable. It had been locked from the other side, becoming, in the process, a doubly sealed door.

This came as a shock, but even more shocking was my discovery of a tiny pencil drawing of a spider that I almost certainly wouldn't have spotted were it not for the fact that it had fifteen legs, which increased the size of the drawing and therefore the visibility of that diminutive arachnid, or symbol of something, whose meaning was entirely beyond me.

The drawing was located in the very middle of the door, level with the rusty lock.

The obvious explanation was that, during my breakfast, someone from the hotel who had a key to my room had taken it upon themselves to move the closet and draw the spider. That it was so tiny and discreet was in itself mysterious. Why would the artist go to the trouble of drawing something so minuscule when they were clearly in a hurry? I left my room and went down the invariably deafening stairs in search of the manager and the anonymous artist. In reception, I asked who else in the hotel, besides me, had a key to Room 205. And then, without waiting for a response, I asked what had happened to Room 206.

"We've been through this before," the manager replied, with the face of someone mustering all his patience. "The sealed door inside Room 205 is blocked off, but since nobody ever listens, we're forced to keep saying it. And in this hotel, both back when it was called the Cervantes and today, Room 206 has always been in the same place, namely no place at all, do you understand? And if Room 206 did disappear at some point, it must have been back in the days of Calle Yerbal, isn't that right?"

This final question was directed at his assistant, who immediately nodded in a way that was both approving and almost lustful, which clearly met with the approval of Manager Mustache. Before asking what he meant about Calle Yerbal, I demanded once more that they open the door to my adjoining room from the inside, but it was no use: that door, they assured me, had always been a door that led nowhere.

But yesterday it was ajar, I said, and I walked through it. A door that leads nowhere can never be ajar, the manager declared with admirable certainty. I decided to change tack, rather than falling into any more verbal traps, and asked about Calle Yerbal and what he'd meant by bringing it up. It's just a saying, he said, stammering a little. Then his assistant took the trouble to explain that it was a street that hadn't existed for a long time. It used to be in the south of the city, not very far from here, the manager said, adding that it had been famous for its brothels, because tango had been invented there at the same time as on Calle Junín in Buenos Aires. When I was in Finland, I said, people in Helsinki told me they were the ones who invented tango. The silence that followed was more terrifying than that of a fat, furry dead spider.

And then the manager, adopting an erudite air, said there was no shortage of people who considered tango "unsavory" because of the disreputable places where it had come into being, although the vast majority danced it enthusiastically among themselves, and you know, my father and my grandfather were both big Gardel fans—aren't you?

I did my best to make him see that we were talking more and more about tango and not at all about the vanished room. And the tension mounted still further when Nicomedes tried to tell me, using his eyes and a range of hand gestures (as if he were speaking to a deaf-mute), that he was the only member of the hotel staff who could give me any pointers about the disappearance. But that set me off wondering what mysterious disappearance he was referring to: that of Gardel on the Medellín airfield or that of Room 206?

What with one thing and another, I was lost. Between the sealed door and that little spider sketch level with the lock and the invention of tango in Finland, plus Nicomedes's incomprehensible gesticulations, I was more disorientated than ever. And since I had no idea how to respond and was in a position of total vulnerability, that dreadful manager dared to suggest that I could quite easily have dreamed my visit to the adjoining room, and that this was the only—he emphasized the word *only*—possibility he could see. Sure, I said, unable to believe that it had come to this. It seemed very rude of him to say that I must have dreamed it. But it was even ruder of him to add, in the face of my stunned silence, that this dream could perhaps have revealed to me "hidden layers, ancestral terrors in my psyche," which surfaced from time to time only by means of the very darkest nightmares.

This is no way to treat a paying guest, was all I managed to say. And he asked if it was because he'd mentioned hidden layers. I had no idea how to respond to that, simply because I was still feeling vulnerable, insecure, indecisive, and shaken up by the disappearance of the adjoining room, and because I had been left speechless, cornered by my surprise at such a brazen attempt by the manager to pry into my life. Because the question, quite clearly, was: Even supposing I had dreamed it, which was absolutely not the case, what could that manager say and know about a dream or nightmare that was utterly inaccessible to him, since it was part of my innermost private life? I even felt like saying to him: What kind of a manager are you, anyway?

3

And indeed, on recent nights I'd lain awake pondering this kind of deep immersion by third parties into other peoples' lives, and what tended to happen when someone wrote a person's biography and talked about their work and their actions and what they said in this or that place and also what people said about them. I knew that the person's life would be diluted, and that a dream they once had, for example, or a particular sensation, a moment of wonder, a glance, all those things would be *much more them* than this more discernible story, the story of their life. A biographer recounting a dream their subject once had, even if the subject had described that dream publicly, would always sound completely nonsensical and end up revealing the limitations of such an undertaking. That was why I enjoyed, in *Nietzsche: A Life,* by Kurt Kobel, which was a distorted biography in the style of David Markson, paragraphs such as this one: "Lying in the grass, Nietzsche contemplated the clouds in the sky, perhaps seeing in those strange forms hippopotami on the way to Jerusalem, or gigantic flying insects. But Nietzsche never told anyone about that."

Meanwhile, I still had the manager in front of me with his talk of "hidden layers." And I felt such an urge to ask him that question—"What kind of manager are you, anyway?"—that in the end I couldn't hold it in any longer. This is the reception desk, we're not management, he shot back, with a kind of abject pride. Then I asked for the hotel bill, fearing I might be charged extra for my impertinence while the League of Suspected Conspirators would get away with theirs scot-free.

I couldn't stand to be around that man a moment longer, much less his bristly laugh that reminded me of the dead spider. For several minutes, getting Big Mustache out of my sight felt even more crucial than unraveling the mystery of the vanished room, which was saying a lot. But I still felt uneasy, as you'd expect, about the sudden absence of Room 206, so I asked if someone could go up to my room and take a look at the sketch of that many-legged spider. I remember feeling convinced that the missing room was still there, whether behind that disused door or floating in some sinister corner of the hotel. And I wondered what Nicomedes really knew about it all. What if he was part of a sect that drove people away if they took an interest in the sealed door, perhaps out of some peculiar aversion to Cortázar? Or the very opposite: it was a sect that worshipped Cortázar and didn't want an intruder, a foreigner, muscling in on their daily rituals.

Even if that association, sect, or secret society existed, or the hotel was hiding a mystery at once unfathomable and terrifying that I had unwittingly walked right into, one indisputable fact remained: Room 206, for all that it had lost its door number and now lived and breathed behind a smooth, white wall, couldn't have turned invisible overnight.

Since none of it made any sense, I couldn't stop asking myself questions, or putting them to everyone else. What if the whole hotel, including Nicomedes, had colluded to make Borges and Gardel continue to prevail over a guest from the past called Julio Cortázar? Nothing quite seemed to fit together, especially not the stuff about Borges. But I felt more and more convinced of the foul atmosphere inside the hotel, and that any investigation that attempted to shed light on it would be like a sealed door and turn out to be a false move on my part.

So, I thought, the sooner I got out of that world of monstrous rotten spider corpses and tiny spider sketches, the better it would be for me. I had to behave, I told myself, as if I hadn't caught on to a thing. That would surely keep me safe, because I didn't entirely trust the situation, and I had no reason to believe those conspirators were upstanding citizens.

However, since I wasn't sure how to go about pretending I knew nothing, I began talking to them about those writers—writers like myself, I specified—who have a congenital defect that keeps them at one remove from experiences. Whenever anything nonanodyne happens in their lives, they withdraw and start asking themselves what it all means and planning how to transform it into a story or novel. Those writers, I said, always have a certain cold impartiality, as if things had nothing to do with them.

I emphasized this last remark, "as if things had nothing to do with them," and I also stressed—as if my life depended on it—the part about "cold impartiality." Once I'd made my point, and after receiving a phone call from Sirés, I hurried up to my room to pack. And as I was packing, I remember, I glanced several times at the closet and the door, as if my gaze could keep them both at bay. But eventually I couldn't resist the call of the darkness any longer, and moved the closet once again to peer through the keyhole of the unusable door. I've never spent such a long time staring through a keyhole without seeing anything. But so transfixed was I by the possibility of seeing something that I grew ever more lost in that deep black expanse. And in the end what I saw was myself on the plane back to Barcelona, as if I'd slowly lifted a piece of carbon paper and found beneath it the exact copy of what would happen to me the next day.

The next day, after sleeping in the hotel arranged by the Centro Cultural, where I'd stayed on first arriving in the city, I got up early and walked down the Rambla Sur, alongside the Río de la Plata. It was a moment of great happiness: strolling next to the open river, far from that inscrutable gang in the Esplendor reception. When Sirés came to pick me up for lunch, I didn't say anything about what had happened, partly because I imagined that, reasonably enough, he wouldn't believe me, which would complicate the situation still further: it would be terrible, considering how hamfisted he was, if he tried to solve the mystery himself by going back to the Esplendor.

I had lunch with Sirés, who also invited along some other participants in the Centro Cultural de España's literary events, such as María Negroni, Fernanda Trías, Philippe Claudel and his wife, and Pablo Silva Olazábal, a writer preparing to publish a collection of interviews with his late friend Mario Levrero, who'd passed away almost ten years before. The chosen place was the restaurant Viejo Sancho, downtown. And what I remember most clearly is that Silva recommended to me several secondhand bookshops, which in the end I couldn't go to because the lunch ran on for so long that we were almost late for the interview.

Once we were on stage in the Estela Medina, Sirés asked me about my work, and as previously agreed, at no point did we mention *Virtuosos of Suspense,* instead spending much of the time on Cortázar's Montevidean tale, which I cited as a perfect example of the kind of story that belongs in category three of my list of narrative trends. The kind of story, I said, that organizes itself around a central obstacle, some impediment that prevents it from telling the reader everything that takes place, meaning that the story remains incomplete, as all stories ultimately do.

As I spoke, I deliberately gave a misleading impression of myself, going overboard in my efforts to make everyone think I was the sort of writer to whom extraordinary things happened but who then approached them in writing with a certain distance, a kind of cold impartiality, as if they had nothing to do with him. And I explained how this was a kind of unconscious defense mechanism that all these writers carry with them wherever they go. Such a writer might, I said, be railing furiously at his girlfriend, while she rages back, at which point he abruptly stops and asks: "Do you mind if I write about this?" With the following reaction from her: "Haven't you been listening to anything I've been saying? Are you even genuinely angry?" To which he might respond that yes, he's livid, but there's still a part of him that's taken up with the question of how it all ought to feel, *really feel,* and even at that very moment he's wondering how to describe the scene, including his reflections about how it ought to feel, which for him is a matter of great importance.

Cold impartiality became the key concept I used to explain that I was the kind of person who always experiences what happens to them from a distance, so as to think about how to describe it later, should I choose to do so. It was like having a sixth sense, I said, which kept me at one remove from the things that happened to me. The aim of all this, of course, was to communicate to any possible spies sent by "the suspects" that they could breathe easy, that I was planning to take my secret with me to Barcelona, and that

I would never reveal that I'd experienced such strange happenings in the Barrio de las Artes.

And then, just minutes after the interview was over, there I was with my luggage standing next to the taxi that would take me to the airport. Sirés had been determined to join me, but I dissuaded him; I felt an overwhelming urge to be alone and mull over what had happened. The car soon turned onto the Rambla Sur. Suddenly, and I could barely believe it, I saw Nikt by the sea—I had no doubt it was him—in agitated conversation with Nicomedes. They seemed to be arguing about something as if their lives depended on it. Were they both, then, part of a secret society? What kind? One that defended itself against the European intellectuals who came to Montevideo in search of a key? Or were Nikt and Nicomedes simply quarreling over something banal that had nothing to do with me? Or had they been planning to murder me that night, thinking I'd be staying once again in the Centro Cultural de España hotel, which wasn't far from where they were standing? I wanted to imagine the ideal scenario: that they'd perhaps been in the audience at the Estela Medina and had left feeling less worried about what I might reveal. But they didn't look remotely reassured at that moment, arguing feverishly right there on the Rambla, and only confirming my suspicion that there was something fishy going on—as fishy as the Río de la Plata behind them.

I was glad I'd pretended to have no intention of capitalizing on that inexplicable and therefore terrifying disappearance of an entire hotel room. I was better off treading carefully, since it seemed to be a serious business, so serious that my life might well be at risk. Because "the suspects" might, at best, be an angelic association who worshipped Cortázar and simply didn't want any more fans in their club. But at worst—it didn't bear thinking about. Perhaps they were the first ever world experts in silent crimes that don't make it into the penal code: hotel room disappearances.

The taxi carried on alongside the river as I pondered what had happened over the past few hours, almost certain that this story of an entire disappearing room would torment and obsess me for a long time to come. Pursuing me in a way that might end up resembling the plot of Cortázar's story "The Pursuer," in which Johnny Carter, alias Charlie Parker, searches compulsively for a way of explaining a mystery: the mystery of the universe. Or, failing that, for a reality that goes beyond real time, a supra-reality in which he might find the meaning of his existence.

One of my final memories of that taxi ride to the airport is the desperate need I felt to get on with *erasing a path,* a journey to Montevideo that had sent me a long way from the "lost lane" before bringing me closer to it.

And just as I was saying that to myself, a voice on the car radio announced "Summertime" sung by Charlie Parker, of whom Johnny Carter was such a sad reflection. It was a chance occurrence, something I knew by then wasn't always mere coincidence, but at the same time it was so relevant to the thoughts filling my head that I didn't want to grope around for any meaning behind it. Why should I? An explanation would ruin everything. Instead, I was going to leave Montevideo without a plausible rationale for the goings-on inside the Esplendor.

But the truly dreadful thing about that taxi ride was the momentary shock of finding that I really had become that man with his *cold impartiality,* the very person I'd tried to pretend I was. Because when I thought back to that monstrous giant spider on top of the red suitcase, I finally had to admit that, much as I'd tried to deceive myself to make the experience less awful, that spider with its four pairs of legs had in fact been alive, very much alive, and I had known it perfectly well. And then I found myself thinking that really it was none of my business, which I found truly horrifying, simply because it showed I was able to persuade myself that it had nothing to do with me.

5

Just a few days after returning to Barcelona, I was pleased, as always, to receive a phone call from Mario Desdini, the son of a good friend of mine and a young student at the Orsay Mathematical Institute in Paris. He came to the city from time to time to see his parents, and occasionally he'd arrange to meet me for a chat—"to talk for talking's sake," he'd add.

We always met at the Bérgamo, on the corner of Calle Mallorca and Rambla de Cataluña. It was a bar I'd heard had been one of Juan Rulfo's regular haunts during his stays in the city and that I liked to visit partly for the same reasons Kobel had visited Einstein's old home in Berne: to see if he could absorb even the tiniest drop of the man's immense and inexhaustible talent.

During one of my encounters with the young Desdini, I'd told him the story of the Princeton mathematicians, brilliant men who retired at forty and spent their time reading the *Divine Comedy*. During another, I revealed the existence of OuLiPo, the scientific and literary society, which he'd never heard of before and found fascinating. At other times, he was the one who told me about unsolvable math problems, and although I didn't feel as if I understood much, what I did understand always proved very useful.

Once again, we met in the Bérgamo. And since we hadn't seen each other for a year and I was still silently affected by the "seemingly unsolvable problem" of Montevideo, I told him, first, how I'd walked around that city, sometimes with a Catalan man called Sirés, who had taken me to the Tower of Panoramas, and sometimes with no one at all, alone and happy by the sea, but how I'd then—and here I swore him to secrecy—roamed the corridors and staircases of a labyrinthine hotel full of people who, though they didn't admit it, clearly formed part of a society of conspirators and wanted something from me, though I never found out what, and how in the end I'd thought it better to take no chances and escape the whole tiresome mess.

With that, I decided to ask—knowing that his response would be helpful, however much or little of it I understood—if he thought there was any chance of escaping, of finding a way out, for example, of the mental maze that had taken over my brain since Montevideo, although, not wanting to complicate things further, I didn't mention that the monstrous spider in the adjoining room had been alive.

At that moment, in the Bérgamo, Marianne Faithfull could be heard in the background singing "No Moon in Paris." And when the young Desdini told me that this was the song that had most helped him to think in his life and, as a result, to feel sad, and therefore to "let go" when it came to setting out math problems, my expectations were high.

I think I can explain something to you, he said, and with

his permission, I recorded his response. Random walks involve walkers deciding to move at random through a given maze. The interesting question is: Do they always return to the starting point, or do they manage to escape? It's a question that's often easy to answer, because there are just two competing forces: one is the geometry of the maze, and the other is the random nature of the walk. The idea is that, when the walker returns to the origin, the game begins again and the past is forgotten, so that the probability of returning x times to the origin is the same as the probability of x walkers in the same maze returning to the starting point, the origin, once. This Russian-doll nature of things simplifies the calculations considerably. If the walker has no preference for any particular direction and the maze is a single line or plane, they'll end up returning to the starting point, but if the maze has three dimensions, they'll end up escaping. The Earth, like a sheet of paper, could be seen as a two-dimensional object, since there are just two degrees of freedom (we can't fly through the air). Now let's look at the same problem, but in reverse: the maze is random and the path is not. It's a more complicated problem, but well worth considering. The idea is to take a labyrinth, spiderweb, or electrical circuit and erase paths with a certain probability. The question is the same: whether the walker escapes or remains trapped, which will depend only on the geometry and the probability of *erasing a path*.

It seemed miraculous, or like the most carefully calibrated science—and also, of course, quite momentous—that Desdini had spoken of *erasing a path*. And I thought that this coincidence was a sign that my route to the "lost lane" was beginning to be restored.

6

Just two days later, an email from an illuminated Madeleine Moore landed in my inbox in Barcelona. "I find myself right next to the Nevsky Prospekt and a few yards from the home, now a museum, of the Nabokov family, in Saint Petersburg. The city still has something, or indeed a great deal, of what Andrei Bely describes in his 1916 novel *Petersburg:* an almighty city, a cracked-open urbe full of gaps and holes, a metropolis with a shadowy, sibylline mouth through which hell itself speaks. I feel extremely inspired here. I'm noticing what some people call a 'flow state.' Will you be in Barcelona next Saturday? If so, we could meet in the morning and discuss your contribution to my upcoming retrospective at the Beaubourg. Do you know why we call the Pompidou the Beaubourg? After the museum opened to the public, Baudrillard coined the phrase *Beaubourg effect* in an article lampooning it as a space set up to embrace mass culture and contain a pure simulacrum as a model of civilization. And the name stuck. After all, Pompidou sounded very funereal, and what's more, it began with the syllable *pomp,* so that it wasn't just the surname of a politician but also evoked funeral pomp. So I'm with those who prefer to call it the Beaubourg, even if it's intended ironically. Anyway, I wanted to tell you that I'm going to Madrid on Wednesday, and then, on my way back to Paris by train, I could stop in Barcelona and meet you in the bar of your choice. I'd like you to take part somehow in the show I'm preparing. Goodbye and поцелуи (that is, 'kisses' in Russian)."

Although I didn't know exactly what it would involve, Moore's proposal seemed no less stimulating than the others she'd made me in the past. I always enjoyed taking part in her projects, and this time it might even help me overcome my Rimbaud syndrome, though I wasn't sure how much I still wanted to do that. Nothing pleased me more than participating, always very indirectly, in the "expanded literature" of the great Madeleine Moore.

7

Saturday came around and close to noon I found myself with Moore in the Belvedere, the bar near the La Central bookshop, in Barcelona. As I'd expected, she was interested in the story—which I told in full and without hiding the fact that the gigantic spider had been alive—of Room 205 and the overnight disappearance of Room 206, along with the rest of my experiences at the Esplendor in Montevideo. What I'd been through, she said, seemed related to the Splendide, the one-room hotel she was designing in order to house, within the Beaubourg, the retrospective of her work: *Madeleine Moore, 1887–2058.*

With my best smile, I asked if she'd really been born in 1887. Have you lived through so much, Moore? Well, she said, '87 was one of the years when "world's fairs" were taking place in Europe, and also the year Marcel Duchamp was born. And *2058,* as you know, was the title of the great apocalyptic show by Dominique (González-Foerster, her friend), in the Turbine Hall at the Tate Modern.

Moore was planning to bring together all her years of work and display it across various stands in her Splendide, with the hotel's solitary "only room" in the exact center, carefully closed off, removed from everyone's gaze. The number of that room would be 19—a direct reference, she said, to a British movie from 1950 that had always intrigued her: *So Long at the Fair,* by Terence Fisher, starring Jean Simmons and Dirk Bogarde.

That movie, which in Spain had been called *Extraño suceso,* or *Strange Occurrence,* was about a hotel room that disappeared overnight in a thoroughly mysterious way. The action centered around a young English girl and her brother who traveled to Paris for the World's Fair in 1889, each taking a room in a luxurious hotel, only for the girl to discover, the morning after their arrival, that the room where her younger brother had slept, Room 19, had quite literally vanished without a trace, and what was more, everyone in the hotel denied the existence of this brother and, indeed, that there had ever been a Room 19.

It was difficult, Moore said, to turn a blind eye to the parallels between my stay at the Esplendor in Montevideo and *So Long at the Fair.* Perhaps the sole room in her Splendide, she said, would bring back the disappeared room in Montevideo and in the process, she smiled, the one in the British movie.

And besides, she added, what are the chances of such a rare event taking place in both hotels, yours and the one in the movie? A coincidence isn't always down to chance, I replied. And then I brought up that relationship between two things that sometimes, according to Sebald, glimmers through a threadbare piece of cloth. But either I didn't explain it very well—which was most likely because, as with the *unnarratable* episode in Almería, I wasn't qualified to describe things I found inexplicable—or, worse, I explained it thoroughly ineptly.

"Well, it's also strange that, even with so many miles between us over the last three months," I said, trying to tackle the conundrum in the most rational way, "we both struck on such similar stories."

"But mine," said Moore, "only happened in a movie. Yours, meanwhile, is a serious matter. And with a live spider involved."

8

When I least expected it, Moore told me about her idea, which she'd been planning for a while, she said, and which the goings-on in Montevideo had only made her more determined to set in motion: I would be the sole person with access to that room in the Splendide. There would be a key and it would be for me alone, a key that would arrive at my apartment by registered mail, a week before the opening, which, of course, I was expected to attend.

I couldn't help thinking of the key I'd heard about in Montevideo, which all the European intellectuals looked for in Paris. And I asked Madeleine if she would have a copy of my room key. Yes, I will, she said, and joked: in case you get locked in. And as soon as I heard that, I laughed as well, feeling my anxiety about taking part in the retrospective escalate, although at the same time a famous verse by Rimbaud from *Illuminations* crossed my mind:

"I alone hold the key to this wild parade."

I couldn't help it, perhaps because I still saw *Virtuosos of Suspense* and the Rimbaud syndrome as part of my personal heritage: with a sudden rush of humility, and I would also say of absolute poetic justice, I thought quite sincerely that it was Rimbaud and not me, never poor old me, who deserved to be inside that room.

And what would Rimbaud do in the hotel's only room? asked Moore. I thought for a while. You're right, I said, what would he do? And what could Rimbaud possibly do by himself in a room in a museum that had been designed exclusively for you? she asked. Right now I don't know, I said, confused, pulling the faces of a man whose head was in a minor—but increasingly major—muddle.

You've reminded me of the elderly Rimbaud, said Moore, the bewildered old man Le Clézio describes in *The Quarantine*. I don't know the book, I said. On a stopover in Aden, or perhaps Harar, she said, the aging Rimbaud went into a tavern, now a pathetic, rootless figure, with fierce but anemic eyes, and alone, tremendously alone, because he lacked the company of literature—a wreck at death's door who used to poison the starving dogs that roamed the city.

I didn't know how to break free of the tangle I'd gotten myself into by wanting Rimbaud, the epicenter of a book that had pursued and aggrieved me for so long, to take my place in that fantastic proposal Madeleine had made me. Even so, I still believed, deep down, that Rimbaud ought to be in the only room in that hotel. But why? Because I had seen him *alive,* one evening, at the entrance to the Pont des Arts. I decided to tell Madeleine: I thought I'd seen him late on a winter's afternoon, standing straight-backed and almost motionless, probably high and looking like he was on another planet, or on no planet at all, at the very foot of the bridge, seemingly engrossed in contemplating the Île de la Cité.

Seeing him there like that, I said, hadn't been particularly surprising, since after all, he had expressed how much he'd like people to realize that, after so many years on another continent, he'd become a different ethnicity. I asked Moore if she knew about that. Not a thing, she said. Well, that was the reason, I said, why Rimbaud had ended up saying that he wouldn't mind being literally exhibited in a Parisian square.

I had always connected that request of his to the great European euphoria of "world's fairs." Because Rimbaud, without knowing it, was simply asking to be exhibited *in the same way that,* back then, in Madrid, thatched huts were imported from the Filipino rainforest and *live* "ethnic specimens"—seminaked natives from that country, from the island of Luzon I believe—plonked down in front of them, an exhibition that today would spark an almighty furor.

The way I see it, I went on, offering him the hotel's only room would remind everyone of that desire of his, expressed in Harar, to be *exhibited.*

"Absolutely not!" Moore exclaimed, very theatrically. "You must not have heard what a sight Rimbaud was when he returned. So I'm afraid you'll have to give in and accept being the only person who has a key to the only room in the Splendide. And I'd say yes if I were you, because you won't have another opportunity like this. Now that you're not writing, it could change your life."

I thought of all the times I'd queued up outside the Beaubourg, sometimes not even making it through the doors. And now, I thought, I was being offered a bedroom inside the museum—a real step forward.

Fine, I said. Have it your way, but only because I'm nice.

9

Whether he was alive or dead, and whether or not he was Rimbaud, that wild, aimless young man I'd seen *alive* on the Pont des Arts, the main thing, as far as I was concerned, was that with his *Je est un autre*—a line from a letter, a line so mythologized when it could just have been a simple slip of the pen—he had transformed the notion of identity for so many of us. Moore then asked if this was why I was so keen for her to exhibit the poet in the middle of a room made of glass, a hall of mirrors that would show us an array of Rimbauds, multiple Rimbauds, shooting out in multiple directions.

Unless I was mistaken, I said, putting it to her straight, at no point had she mentioned a glass room. Just then, I'll always remember, a piercing ray of sunshine burst into the Belvedere, and something totally unexpected happened. The hotel's only room, she replied, suddenly angry, and as if that ray of sunshine had redoubled her energy, wasn't intended for exhibiting anyone, not even the living Rimbaud, but for exactly the opposite. As my friend, she'd been dreaming up that solitary place, that sole room, just for me, ever since she'd first noticed, to her alarm, that not writing was turning me into a deceased Rimbaud.

I couldn't believe my ears. There was nothing I hated more than the word *deceased,* and she couldn't claim not to have known that.

"Besides," she said, "as your friend, I think it would do you good to get to know your true room and reflect on it deeply, and also to search, if the opportunity arises, for a door that might lead you to a new place and a new book—the only way, I guarantee you, of keeping death at bay."

10

I was in no way reassured to hear her mention a door when I was still seeing, in fitful nightmares, both the door that had disappeared in Montevideo and the one that had been locked from the inside, imprisoning the monstrous spider. What's more, that door reminded me of what I'd been told was written in *Hopscotch:* that there was a certain kind of European intellectual who sensed that somewhere in Paris there was a key and searched for it like a madman.

Seeing my disconcerted expression, Moore quickly changed the subject. You'll be pleased, she said, perhaps even delighted to hear that the hotel's only room won't have any adjoining rooms whatsoever. At the most you'll have Luc Bouchez, but a long way away. Luc will be working on a sound and music composition that resembles the voice we hear inside our heads when we think.

I wondered what this internal voice Luc Bouchez was working on could possibly sound like, when I, for one, wouldn't have recognized so much as the timbre of my own. And as I mulled it over, I can clearly remember, the minutes were going by, and then the hours, the days, and soon the weeks and months—in old movies it would be pages of a calendar wafting away—and that day in the Belvedere gradually faded into the past and I remained stuck in my habit of never writing a single line, whether of fiction or essays, not a single line, always waiting for the moment when, perhaps without even realizing, I'd put my pen to the blank page and set down some initial phrases that would mark the end of my writer's block. Although, now and then, I expected the opposite: a continuation of the contented, peaceful, bland routine life of a person who dispenses entirely with the written word and instead fills his time with a constant stream of trivial activities.

11

Months later, after plenty more calendar pages had blown away, I was disembarking at Austerlitz station, in Paris, to attend the opening of Moore's retrospective. The moment I set foot on the platform, I saw someone I knew, also from Barcelona, who expressed surprise that I wasn't publishing with the same manic frequency as before. I wanted to tell him that just recently I'd been in St. Gallen, at a conference whose grandiloquent name I abbreviated in my head to "the Ambiguity Conference," and that I therefore wasn't short of things to keep me busy and was managing, moreover, to feel that writing was something I could live without. But that acquaintance, who has a reputation in Barcelona for interrupting everyone and their dog, cut me off before I could even mention St. Gallen.

Then I remembered Lisa Barinaga in Lisbon and how I'd answered her as if I were Duchamp. And I decided to press on with that approach, to see if the game of *Je est un autre* would work any better this time. It wasn't so hard: I simply had to react quickly when someone asked if it was true I'd stopped writing and answer them as a person other than myself, choosing for this imposture whomever I'd been reminded of by the tone of the question. And the tone of that Barcelona man's question in Austerlitz station was so lugubrious that I decided to turn into H. P. Lovecraft.

After all, I'd always wanted to get inside the skin of that writer from Providence, who from a very tender age, ten years old, had been fascinated by astronomy, so much so that he thought of nothing else, though with the particularity that what most interested him about that science was not to be found within the Solar System.

That day, at Austerlitz station, with a firm and deliberately sinister air, I ran my index finger across my throat.

"I hate ink," I said to the man from Barcelona. "I have a problem with it, because it's black like the blood in our neck and as dark as the universe."

"I wasn't asking for explanations," he replied, in the process revealing that he was still one of those people who believed in them.

Then I hurried away, happy to have turned into Lovecraft for a few moments and happy, too, to have shaken off the man from Barcelona. I went in search of a taxi, checking I still had with me the key to the only room in the Splendide, the key I felt so proud of, among other things because it was an homage to Unica, which means "only" in Spanish and was famously the brand of the lock and key to the cellar in *Notorious,* that magnificent Hitchcock film.

A rainy day in Paris, for a change. The taxi took me down various avenues and boulevards, and half an hour later, after some horrendous traffic, I arrived at the Hôtel Le Littré on Rue Littré with just enough time to change my clothes before rushing back out in search of another taxi that would take me to the Beaubourg, which, if it's not too ridiculous a comparison, I approached with similar enthusiasm to Stendhal, who, the moment he arrived in Milan, set off in pursuit of that essential thing, the one that dictates so many of our actions and which we deem the highest of all pleasures (music, in his case): "I arrive exhausted at seven o'clock in the evening. I run to the Scala. My journey was justified, etc."

Someone has commented that in that moment Stendhal was like a maniac who arrived in a city a slave to his passions and that very night quite literally raced out to the pleasure spots he had identified. And yes, it was true: there really was something manic about him, and the image of him haring off to the Scala confirmed how disfigured we can be by the pursuit of pleasure, perhaps because the signs of fanatical passion are always incongruous, minuscule, trifling, just as the objects of such passion are usually quite unexpected.

In my case, instead of that irresistible Italian music, the only sign of my passion that evening in Paris was the Unica-branded key, which had arrived in Barcelona as promised by registered mail and which, even in the taxi, I kept checking was still in my pocket, knowing that this key would let me into a room in the Beaubourg that Moore had designed especially for me, perhaps the "authentic room," that *das eigentliche Zimmer* (the true room) that Robert Walser spoke of in one of his microscripts.

12

As soon as I was inside the Beaubourg, I ran into Moore and her boyfriend and began to walk with them around the elaborate retrospective, following a route that seemed at times to be endless and which I thought might turn out to be entirely circular and therefore inexhaustible. In a way, it was a kind of premonition of what lay in store for me in the hotel's only room.

We passed the door to Room 19 several times, and at no

point—which struck me as extremely odd—did Moore give the slightest indication that it was my room, my true room, or my *only* room, as she called it.

It was as if we had all the time in the world, as if Room 19 remained unfinished or simply didn't yet exist. And so, when Madeleine and René became embroiled in an animated discussion with Luc Bouchez and the writer Pierre Testard, I seized my chance to slip off, to get as far away from Bouchez as possible, though at that point it hadn't occurred to me that he might later become my neighbor. Without wasting a second, I headed for Room 19, tremendously curious to find out what awaited me inside.

But my eagerness soon turned into two opposing feelings. On the one hand, an explosion of happiness. And on the other, a premonition of failure, a justifiable terror at being about to discover what every "French writer," because of their proverbial closeness to lucidity, ends up glimpsing sooner or later: the impossibility of committing to paper the boundless intensity of a personal joy.

It's one of the great moments in the literature of his century. The young Stendhal, known in those days as Marie-Henri Beyle, discovers total happiness, but as he writes, his prose, as a direct consequence of such good fortune, dissolves into disconnected words, mutterings, random exclamations, and half-finished thoughts. This shouldn't be surprising. After all, what can a writer say about that which leads him beyond absolute fulfillment? All that remains is to attempt to gather up those words, avoiding, as far as possible, any faltering that might unleash a torrent of stuttering and stammering. But if, despite everything, this does come about, the writer, ordinarily so fussy about his syntax, must accept utter defeat.

In a kind of parallel story to that of Stendhal in Milan, though with obvious differences, I approached door number 19 in the Beaubourg that day feeling happy and expectant, only to be thoroughly disappointed, on opening it with my Unica key, by the sight of a darkness so thick that I couldn't see anything, or indeed go any farther. Not even a Stendhalian stammer was an option, because it was the most easily describable interior I'd ever encountered in my life, and didn't grant the viewer the slightest possibility of failing to put it into words.

Had this really been designed for me? My first thought was that Madeleine Moore hadn't forgiven me for my potential misgivings about *La concession française* and this was her way of getting revenge, both for what she suspected I thought of her book and for my inexplicable tirade against inner worlds. It was as if she were telling me: "So you don't believe in those worlds? Well, here's one of them. Full, yes, of inner darkness, but just assume you can't see anything because there's nothing there. It's yours."

13

I couldn't even find a light switch and didn't dare step forward in case I tumbled headfirst onto the tiles, the door slammed shut behind me, and—exaggerating now, for a bit of a laugh—I died right there in the middle of the Beaubourg. My fear of being trapped inside that camera obscura meant that for several seconds I didn't move from the doorway.

But nothing lasts forever. As the light timidly spread through the real room, I began to see there was something inside, though just as I thought I was about to find out what it was, I felt, as if set off by a spring perhaps activated by my own Unica key, a warm wind that carried with it a mist, a wind I soon saw was quite clearly artificial but which days later I realized even had a name. It was called *foehn,* it blew in Bavaria, and it was the final word of a novel that John Ashbery had written with James Schuyler, *A Nest of Ninnies.* Ashbery had found it particularly amusing to end the novel with a word, *foehn,* that his readers wouldn't know, so that if they wanted to find out the meaning they would have to open a dictionary—that is, close one book only to open another.

When the mist from the *foehn* had cleared, the sole object in the room gradually came into view, located almost in the very center: a red suitcase. It wasn't the suitcase from Montevideo, but it wasn't far off: this one, too, was old-fashioned, of a similar size and with a very similar handle. And although the joke, on Moore's part, could have struck me as a little inappropriate, I was at least grateful that, since she knew the whole story of my time in the Esplendor, she'd been kind enough to spare me the enormous spider.

Thank you, Madeleine, for skipping the live spider, I murmured. At the far end of the room was another door.

Was that it? A suitcase and a door at the far end that I couldn't open? If so, I could leave my room now, because I'd seen all there was to see. But then, to my surprise, there came that voice we hear inside our own heads when we think, in this case presumably created by Luc Bouchez.

Although for a while I'd been unable to remember what the voice in my head was like, and wasn't even sure I'd ever heard it, I ended up recognizing it as if I'd been hearing it all my life. Not only was it a very good imitation of my own voice, but it kept saying things that sounded familiar, because I'd written them at different stages of my life. Phrases

I recognized with genuine displeasure, since they dated back to unfortunate moments from the past. Did Madeleine want me to hear, in that room, the most "select" examples of all that I'd written over the years? If so, it was a completely preposterous idea and I wouldn't be able to stand it, because I'd written an awful lot.

There came a break in the sentences, many of which I'd composed without a second thought, but I couldn't enjoy it for long because just then a chorus of voices burst in:

"Yes, you've written a lot."

"This is the final straw," I said out loud, trying to keep my dignity and be a good sport, and also to banish as far as possible that meddlesome, ghostly Greek chorus. The silence that followed, I noticed, had been recorded in advance, that is, it had been calculated, planned as a pause.

"Are you lost souls or sons of bitches?" I asked, in the style of Valle-Inclán in *Ballad of Wolves*. And the choir remained silent, making way for a return of that inner voice produced by Bouchez, which soon explained that this only room in the hotel was an austere re-creation of that much-feared hell, about which all we know is that it goes round and round and is circular in shape, and almost unbearable in nature.

The room, without a doubt, was aiming to resemble that famous, fiery, and terrible realm which the Christian Devil keeps in some secret location and which we know as hell, only without the screams of rage, without the murmurs and moans. There were no sighs, no sobs, no laments, no howls, but I was quite clearly in that place where writers are condemned to hear for all eternity the soundtrack of everything they ever wrote in their lives. An infinite, infernal torment.

"You are in Bogotá," said the voice.

14

I began to wonder, alarmed, how long this rather confrontational recording of Moore's might last. How long had she planned for me to spend listening to this series of statements, so many of them foolish or vile and all of them mine—as much mine as that only room? What I couldn't understand was why Moore had worked so hard to bring about something so unpleasant. Because being faced with that infernal Bogotá, even if you managed to take a step back and see it as a twisted joke, was like a bullet to the head, like instant suicide.

Not wanting to waste any more time, I called Moore on her mobile to ask what *all that* had been about. Since she was surrounded by so many people at the opening, I didn't expect her to answer, let alone as quickly as she did. I told her I was now in the only room and wanted to know whom the red suitcase belonged to and why there was nothing else in there and why the door out didn't open.

And, well, I quickly corrected myself, there is something else: the whole time I'm hearing the worst sentences I've ever written in my life.

"Yes, you've written a lot," the chorus repeated.

The suitcase belonged to Marlene Dietrich, Moore answered without missing a beat. It was a present the actress had received from Josef von Sternberg after filming *Shanghai Express*. I pretended to remain impassive in the face of what I'd heard and even thought she'd told it to me simply so she could say the word *Shanghai*, something I knew she loved to do. There was a brief silence, which I broke by telling her that the suitcase was as nasty and objectionable as the room itself, and then I asked if she'd devised the whole thing in order to destroy me. Another silence, followed by more questions from me: Was her intention that I'd attempt to get out of there by means of the adjoining room? Because if so, I said, the adjoining room is locked.

Another silence. Then Moore's voice again:

"I thought you were all out of ideas?"

15

Then came the sound of torrential rain, ferocious rain, as if all the water from all the planet's seas were falling onto hell. An acoustic effect. And indeed, for years it had been the watermark (a particularly apt term) of all Madeleine Moore's "artistic acts." It was an effect she called "tropical-ization," and ever since she began spending long periods in Rio, staying with her friend Dominique, it tended to be part of her work.

I don't know how long I spent hypnotized by the noise of that downpour and the feeling that the world existed only when I perceived it, though it also seemed possible that the world existed at the edge of my own being, which in this case could only be because there was always someone else perceiving it, since otherwise there would be no world, or stars, or universe, or paranoia of any kind. The question that gave rise to this feeling was the same one I'd heard Michi Panera ask himself so many times: Are we in the land of the living or somewhere else?

"You are in Bogotá," the voice reminded me once more.

And for me, it was as if it had said: you are in the land of the dead. There was no other city in the world whose name could distress me more, because in Bogotá I'd had a pretty rough time of it. I'd accepted the invitation to visit the city so as to escape the hell that my personal life in Barcelona had become, only to realize, as soon as I arrived, that I had ended up in a hell of far greater proportions.

For one thing, I encountered a city under siege, something that no one had warned me about in the airport in Madrid and that I had in no way expected, though admittedly at first I found it quite exciting when it was hinted that it was due to problems with the guerrillas. However, the real reason for that siege was more prosaic and completely unprecedented for me: the census would be taken the next day, and the population, in preparation for being visited by civil servants, had to remain at the addresses where they were registered.

As a result, early the next morning I would see a Bogotá that was completely deserted, the first city I had ever seen in that state, with almost no one out of doors, only groups of police officers on motorcycles patrolling the streets—some of which were known as *carreras,* i.e., avenues—and conjuring up images of *Blade Runner.* In Plaza de Bolívar, next to the big plaza outside the cathedral, there was no one to be seen, aside from two convivial drunks cursing the president.

The day before, at the airport, it took a long time to resolve the problem of my not having a permit to enter the city. I'd described that nerve-wracking ordeal to Moore on several occasions, which had in the end inspired her to create that hell inside Room 19, so very exclusively made for me and so very, very tedious.

It was a long and laborious process, getting that permit,

and eventually I was driven—after all, I was an official guest, one of the judges of a national prize for unpublished Colombian fiction—in a police car that went rattling over a series of potholes until it reached the skyscraper on Carrera 10 called the Royal Orchid; the old Hilton, I was told. A hotel with lots of rooms, though almost none of them was occupied, which seemed odd. In the mornings there were very few guests in the big breakfast room on the ground floor, the same room where, on the night of my arrival, I had read that ironic headline in *El Tiempo:* "Census tomorrow—to see how many of us are left."

The fact that almost no one else was having breakfast there obsessed my two fellow judges (both Mexican) and their respective partners, and it obsessed me as well. But the oddest thing about that ghostly skyscraper was the fact that every time we returned to the hotel and got into the elevators, we always had to do so in the company of sullen, silent police officers in charge of dogs that sniffed us eagerly, searching, we imagined, for gunpowder as well as cocaine.

16

Throughout my time in that city, taking a walk around the downtown, strolling as far as the nearby Plaza de Bolívar, always felt as strange as it did dangerous. Not even in the company of the two Mexican judges, who were tall and solidly built, did I feel safe, since danger in its various forms—these were the final days of the previous century, when the conflict in Colombia was at its peak—lurked around every corner and made me feel constantly on edge, and because the visual horror was enough to affect even the most hardened local. During that time, I remember, there was endless talk of child murderers, hired to kill for tiny sums of money and known by the unforgivable name of "the disposables."

You thought you saw those children all over the place, just as outside every store you'd see a security guard who clearly wouldn't lift a finger if you got into trouble. Further contributions to the visual horror came from the beggars and madmen who followed you around like sleepwalkers with blank, staring eyes. All quite harmless, but on first sight very alarming.

One surprising, terrifying, Hitchcockian detail from my stay in Bogotá has particularly stuck in my mind. We'd been in the hotel for three days and had gotten used to being whisked straight up in the elevator to the very top floors, where almost all of the smattering of guests were staying, when one of the elevators came to an unexpected halt at the fifth floor, where it had never stopped before. There was an instant of mute, icy terror, which lasted only long enough for the metal doors to open and shut, revealing what was buried there in the bowels of the building: the offices of the Ministry of Justice, hidden away on that floor after the whole of the previous ministry building, on Plaza de Bolívar, had been attacked by urban guerrillas from the M-19, the 19th of April Movement, and in the ensuing commotion had been burned to the ground, although, we were told, no one ever knew for sure who had started the fire. To protect it as far as possible from further attacks, the ministry had been moved to the Royal Orchid, the "comfortable hotel" where we'd been put up.

17

Eventually, Bogotá revealed the beauty that so often goes hand in hand with horror. From the day I first detected that beauty, everything looked up. I'd say the turning point was the visit to the National Library arranged for us judges. At first it seemed a boring prospect, spending a morning traipsing dutifully around a place I thought sounded far too official. But that all changed the moment I saw the current library building, white and elegantly simple, designed by Alberto Wills. And it changed even more when we were told that this library, founded in 1777, had been only the second public library in Latin America. An exceptional young guide informed us that it was in the modest little music room where the young García Márquez, already known to his friends as Gabo, a name that arose from the need to shorten his surnames, had taken refuge, along with everyone else who didn't have the five cents to go to a café, in order to study in silence.

As Gabo himself has said, there was one among this handful of evening regulars that he particularly hated: a blustering man with a heraldic nose and Turkish eyebrows, an enormous body and tiny shoes like Buffalo Bill's, who came in every day without fail at 7:00 p.m. and asked them to play Mendelssohn's violin concerto. It was Álvaro Mutis, who for a long time Gabo thought he'd first met "in the idyllic Cartagena de Indias of 1949," years after those evenings he spent studying in the National Library.

Both men believed that this meeting in Cartagena really had been their first, until one afternoon, years later, Gabo heard Mutis make a passing reference to Felix Mendelssohn. It was a revelation that suddenly transported him back to his student days in the empty little music room. "Many years had to go by," Gabo wrote, "until that afternoon in Mutis's house in Mexico City, when without warning I recognized the stentorian voice, the feet of baby Jesus, the trembling hands incapable of passing a needle through the eye of a camel. Damn it, I said to him in defeat, so it was you."

18

"Intelligence can help us find the opening, the eye, the hole, the gap, small as it might be, which lets us escape whatever has us trapped." I've been relying on this piece of paternal advice not only at times of unspeakable distress but also when, having finished writing one of those novels that tended to lead to a dead end, I found it difficult to set the next project in motion. Indeed, my friends would often ask: "And now, after this, what are you going to do?" Which carried on until one afternoon it struck me that the reason I wrote novels was so that, once they were finished, I could get on with what really interested me: the heroic search for a way out of them.

After the "Paris" fragment and my devastating and sometimes, though only sometimes, distressing writer's block, I had the albeit unprovable impression that people had begun conspiring to make me live through stories that would, in the long run, oblige me to write them down, thereby returning me to the "straight and narrow." I put up some resistance but eventually came to see that, whether or not I resisted, I was living through more things in order to write, even if I wasn't writing.

That impression, which came to feel quite natural, helped

and indeed consoled me in that hellish Bogotá behind door 19, by allowing me to hope—though at the same time I longed to be mistaken—that Moore had fabricated this complex situation for me so that, on getting out of it, I'd then talk about what I'd been through, and even feel an overriding urge to write it down.

But for the time being, I said to myself, the best thing to do is to use my head and look for the gap or, failing that, for the tiny "little hole" (as Bioy Casares called it), which will eventually let me escape this Bogotá that has me so thoroughly trapped. Because after all, I went on saying to myself right there in the Beaubourg, I'd managed to escape the other perverse traps laid for me by all the books I'd written, meaning there was no reason why it should be so difficult to find a means of breaking free of that room.

Did I want to escape my "true room"? By now, almost without realizing it, I'd begun calling it simply that, after Robert Walser, perhaps because I felt more and more enthusiastic about the idea that I'd arrived in a very particular space where my true identity would be revealed to me, if it weren't being revealed to me already.

Anyway, the minutes were going by, and all I was managing to discern was that my most authentic self resided in hell and my Walseresque—and therefore presumably sweet and serene—*das eigentliche Zimmer* was, according to Moore, in Bogotá, somewhere between a white, airy library and the ashes of a Ministry of Justice.

This thought made me all the more determined to find an urgent escape from my truth. The only way out was in fact the entrance; that is, there was no other means of escape besides turning back and retracing my steps, in order to leave Bogotá behind. There might be another way out, which would mean the entrance wasn't my only chance of escape, but that possibility relied on my Unica key working in that door on the far side, which seemed to lead to the rest of the retrospective, to the area where Moore, in collaboration with her friend Dominique, had copied that Danish interior made up of four doors, painted by Vilhelm Hammershoi in *Four Rooms.*

And it was odd, I thought, because that Hammershoi masterpiece sometimes reminded me, depending on my mood when I looked at it, of the involuntary pilgrimage I had recently embarked on through certain doors that together formed a corridor. But was that pilgrimage really involuntary? Perhaps because it sometimes seemed to be controlled by a conspiracy operating in the most shadowy of shadowy realms. At other times I seemed fully in control of it myself as I searched for an ancient path I knew very little about, except that it was a footpath that had diverged and taken me with it. Searching for it meant, first of all, trying to return to a time when no one expected stories to make sense and, moreover, when all stories were stripped of even the slightest obligation to do so. I had been searching for it ever since my friend Paco Monge, not long before he died, had said goodbye with these words: "And why not think that, down there, there's also another forest in which names don't have things?"

And I was searching for it, I think, for the sheer pleasure of searching and also in order to one day celebrate, and rightly so, the end of plots, though at the same time it was paradoxical to find myself suddenly inserted into one, adrift in the middle of one, lost in Hammershoi's corridor. But I trusted that, at some point, the plot would come to an end. Or, which amounted to the same thing: that the last sentence of Ferlosio's Cervantes acceptance speech would be realized: "The plot came to a halt and happiness suddenly took over."

19

It all depended on whether my Unica key would also work in the door at the far end and let me into the next room. That seemed a more dignified way out than going back to the door I came in through, which would have meant retracing my steps and walking once more past that red suitcase that so obsessed me.

Cautiously, I approached the door at the far end, only to be seized on and off by Holy Indecision, which made me worry I might be walking the wrong way and toward the final trap, like that mouse in the Kafka fable who's told by the cat that he simply needs to change direction. And then the cat gobbles him up.

Even so, I went on putting one foot in front of the other, and it was as if I were making my way down a lost lane, full of empty rooms.

You are in Bogotá, the chorus interrupted, but now the voices sounded very far away.

That was when I saw, right by the keyhole in the door at the far end, some spidery marks on the wood, rather like scratches left by an animal scavenging around there. When? And what kind of animal? But no, I said to myself, quickly coming to my senses, they're not the marks of a beast but clues, symbols, human signs accumulated over time. And perhaps, when I said that to myself, I was influenced by the conversation I'd had some weeks before with Cuadrelli in St. Gallen, on a topic he knew plenty about because it had been the specialist subject of some private classes he'd given in his Boston days: the inexhaustible history of *Egyptian symbols*.

Those marks—thank goodness—weren't on the doors of my room in Montevideo, I said to myself, and most likely they were just random signs not intended to send me any message at all. Somewhat encouraged by this conclusion, I grew almost entirely convinced that my Unica key would work in that other door as well. But when I gaily tried it, it didn't do a thing, and I felt more cornered than ever. There was nothing left for me in there, and my only option seemed to be to leave Bogotá however I could, amid the deafening racket from the tropical rain that lashed at that hell, or, what amounted to the same thing: to retreat and retreat, attempting to make my way back, with impossible dignity, to the door by which I'd entered Room 19, and then, relinquishing even my pride, beat a hasty retreat.

I was just getting ready to make my escape, though I hadn't moved from the door at the far end, when what I sometimes think of as an invisible meteorite, falling from the pitch-dark sky re-created on that room's precarious ceiling, sent down that divine breath, a thing no one can explain, even to themselves, and which Cuadrelli had referred to not long ago in St. Gallen as the Breath.

20

> In the doorway there whispered a robe of iris silk.
> —Andrei Bely, *Petersburg*

The Breath reminded me that the camera on my phone allowed for nocturnal inspections and also that it had proved, the previous week, to have certain visual capabilities that I'd tried to forget, though to no avail, perhaps because that very Breath—which I could call my Genie, or Guardian Angel, in Christian terms—was looking out for me.

One week earlier, at home in Barcelona at that time of night when a person's life force is at its lowest ebb, I found myself playing with my camera, filming, with infrared night vision—I simply had to select "activate night mode"—various places around the apartment, without running into any surprises, until I stopped in the hallway and my eye was drawn to the small and, to me, always unsettling guest room. In there, I knew from prior experience, if I stared the darkness straight in the eye, a shadow would gradually take shape, which, if I went on staring harder and harder, always gave the impression that it would soon become a fully fledged specter: perhaps a long-forgotten guest paying me a visit from the vast realm of bygone days.

Whenever this had happened before, I'd always left the room just in time. But that day, thanks to "activate night mode," I sensed that I'd almost certainly be able to go further and see something more than a shadow taking shape. I found the courage, or rather the resolve, to see what would happen, knowing I could always leave if I got into too many difficulties.

And so, instead of standing my ground and staring the darkness in the eye, I switched on my phone's night vision and a few seconds later saw what I always ended up seeing, only this time it was taking shape more quickly: that strange presence like a moving shadow, a presence seemingly belonging to one of the occasional guests who had perhaps never left or who were so fond of that room that they returned from time to time, like the foolish ghost from Dickens who, having all the space in the world at his disposal, always returned to the very same room where he had been so unhappy.

Although admittedly, once again, I didn't make it beyond what I usually saw. When the shadow began to appear, I thought I'd better not hang around waiting for it to take on a physical form and instead, maintaining a certain dignity, though not much because there were no witnesses to the scene, got out of there like a shot.

21

Well, I said to myself, if the Breath had reminded me that my phone camera had that state-of-the-art infrared vision and could move through the darkness like the radar on a ship, in search of another reality, there must have been a reason. The Breath didn't do things just for the sake of it. Besides, I was so trapped in Bogotá that I had to try everything I could in my search for a possible way out, for what my father called the opening, the eye, the hole, the gap, which would allow me to escape.

And so, since I was still facing the door at the far end in which my key didn't work, I aimed my camera at it and began filming in "night mode," and a few moments later I discovered the image of a new door, one that was completely invisible to the real world. I'll never forget that moment, or the thrill of at last finding out what it means to discover something: to see in a new way what no one has ever noticed before.

There were two possible exits, then, though one was invisible, unless you used my night camera and saw for yourself the extent to which there were two doors and not one. The first thing I wondered was if the invisible door would also have marks and scratches next to the keyhole. But the invisible door was, in fact, slightly different to the visible one, or perhaps light-years away from it. For a start, it was brand-new, devoid of any backstory, and spotless, with no scratches, marks, Egyptian symbols, traces of scavenging animals, or live spiders.

A new door.

It had to lead somewhere—into Hammershoi's corridor, most likely—but that remained to be seen. It was as if, for the time being, it was simply a door, but any day it might become a book, or an open window overlooking an old Bogotá road, for example: a Colombian road from another century, without any houses on either side, not yet even Colombian, a path on the outskirts, entirely lost in time.

I could have gotten nervous, but the opposite happened: I relaxed and found myself in the same state as a person who wakes up flustered and shocked because they're halfway between *still not quite being who they are* and the suspicion that they have *the chance to be someone else instead,* and even that another portion of their memory is unfolding within them, which, for me personally that day, meant I came to be walking through a crack very similar to the keyhole of that new door, where the mists of the present and the future had become stuck. So immovable were they, in fact, that at that moment I was able to see some busy New York streets I'd strolled down several months before with Enzo Cuadrelli: a small urban maze, near the Eataly Italian market and that famous wedge-shaped skyscraper, the Flatiron Building—a maze that Cuadrelli and I were seamlessly creating with our steps.

Both he and I, as I walked by his side, were like random walkers who had decided to move according to chance through an urban maze that came more solidly into being as we grew ever more lost within it. Although seen from the top of the Flatiron Building, no doubt we were something else: two chess pieces, for example, adrift on the board of a great mathematical problem that posed the question of whether we would ever find our way back to the starting point or otherwise manage to escape.

We had just left the market, after having lunch in a basement restaurant reached by a sinister door that at first appeared hermetically sealed but in fact was there less for soundproofing purposes than to give the underground space the look of a Prohibition era speakeasy. A venue that promised excitement, but only because of its door.

On leaving the restaurant, we had wandered aimlessly for a long while, talking nonstop, at first about the biography of Bartleby, the scrivener of Wall Street, that Cuadrelli had been working on for ages. He had abandoned it, he told me unexpectedly, to turn his efforts to a book about the movement that had arisen from that very Melville story: Occupy Wall Street, which in September 2011 had sealed off Zuccotti Park in Lower Manhattan with the aim of *continuously occupying the New York financial district,* in a clear and visible protest against "corporate greed and the perception of social inequality."

I said that sounded promising but that it was a shame no one was working on demystifying that phrase of Bartleby's, the very words of which had grown so faded over time. Don't worry, he said, in Buenos Aires there are several projects on the go; the city is full of writers, young and old, who've found a reason to put pen to paper: discrediting the "I would prefer not to."

"And how many people's livelihoods depend on bringing that line into disrepute?"

"Oh, the vast majority's," said Cuadrelli, which was perhaps an exaggeration.

The fact that so many people of all ages were engaged in this smear campaign didn't exactly reassure me, I felt obliged to respond. And then I brought up "Nebulous Borders," the conference in St. Gallen to which we'd been invited by our mutual friend, Yvette Sánchez. And on mentioning that, I found myself remembering certain forays into Swiss territory with Yvette, my favorite being one that involved us sitting for a very, very long time on a pew in Basel Minster in silent homage to the tomb of Erasmus of Rotterdam, seen by some as the King of Indecision, although he was surely quite the opposite and in fact made a great success of his decision to remain always between two fires, without taking the side of either the Catholics or the Reformers, which he abandoned only at the very end of his life, safe in the knowledge that he had been independent and free to the last.

That foray of ours into Basel Minster changed some things in my life, but not my habit of living indecisively, which has always sought to follow me wherever I go and, what's more, has always succeeded.

I couldn't say at what point in our walk around the labyrinthine Flatiron District I stopped calling the event "Nebulous Borders" and began calling it the "Ambiguity Conference." But Cuadrelli noticed it happen, and I realized this when, sixty days later, I turned up in St. Gallen without the faintest idea that Cuadrelli, in his paper "Labyrinth Doubts," would surprise me by giving so many accurate—and bordering on private—details of that stroll in the Flatiron District.

22

Really, the visible is no more than the remainder of the invisible. And that's how I came to be watching myself, through a crack similar to the keyhole in the door I was filming with infrared light at that moment in the Beaubourg, as I strolled with Cuadrelli through New York. We were wandering around the outside of the big Eataly market, and then, some time later, months later in fact, he was reading his paper "Labyrinth Doubts" in a lecture theater at St. Gallen University, whose rear door opened onto a magnificent, grandiose early painting by Richter: a painting I had a habit of recalling in my mind's eye.

Needless to say, I was in the audience for Cuadrelli's paper, and my ears pricked up the moment I realized he was describing a moment of indecision on both our parts, but especially mine, during our walk through that Manhattan district.

"Now I'm going to refer to a 'real' example, in inverted commas, partly to privilege that dimension common to both reality and literature and generally known as 'experience,'" said Cuadrelli, before going on to describe how, some months earlier, after having lunch in one of the many restaurants near the Flatiron, "I was walking along with one of the speakers at this conference . . . ."

These last words put me on high alert, and I sat up

straight at the school desk where I was sitting, ready to give my full attention to whatever was going to be said about me. We were wandering, Cuadrelli continued, in no particular direction, when, during an absent-minded silence, my companion informed me, or rather, divulged in a confessional tone, that he too would be taking part in this gathering in St. Gallen, which he called the "Ambiguity Conference," before adding that he felt less and less sure what the word *ambiguity* actually meant, since while in the past it had seemed quite clear as a concept, it had recently been growing murkier by the day, because he came across it all over the place, including when he wasn't expecting it.

After these words, Cuadrelli embarked on a digression, like a kind of respite, perhaps thinking he'd do me a favor and let me relax. And so off he went, or so it seemed, on a tangent, focusing on the circumstances of Raymond Roussel's suicide in Room 224 of the Grand Hotel et Des Palmes in Palermo; circumstances that were investigated years later by Leonardo Sciascia, leading him to the conclusion that "life events always become more complex and unclear, more ambiguous and misleading, that is, the way they *truly* are, when one writes them down."

These words of Sciascia hinted that writing perhaps meant drawing closer to the true nature of things, with all their ambiguities and associated shadows, and reminded me of those extremely famous words of Saint Augustine, when he confessed that he couldn't explain what time was, even though really—a great paradox—he explained it very well. And, though on a far more modest scale, of course, they reminded me of my own words when I said in Manhattan that the concept of *ambiguity* was something I'd always assumed I understood and yet, recently, had been growing ever less clear.

When Cuadrelli described Roussel's suicide in Room 224, he made sure to mention that until a few years ago, the management of the Grand Hotel et Des Palmes had always considered Wagner their most illustrious guest, which wouldn't be so remarkable were it not for the fact that they didn't even take Roussel into account, as if he'd never so much as set foot in the hotel, let alone ended his life there.

Needless to say, this total unawareness of a writer's passage through a hotel inevitably brought to mind the Esplendor in Montevideo and how the people there seemed not to believe, or not to fully believe, or not to have the slightest desire to believe that Cortázar had been a guest in that establishment.

After this Rousselian digression, Cuadrelli returned to his meticulous account of our walk through that district of New York, going back to the moment at which our having called the very idea of ambiguity into question made us indecisive when it came to crossing Fifth Avenue. It was a moment I had no memory of experiencing, but nor could I be sure I hadn't experienced it. In Cuadrelli's version, the cars stopped to let us past, not realizing that the ambiguity unleashed on the scene made us unable to take a single step: "It was as if a kind of hesitation syndrome were pursuing us and had chosen that moment to make us its playthings."

23

Hesitation syndrome!
Just then, thinking of the book I might have written about

the syndrome of those cultivators of Eternal Doubt, I felt even more regretful about having focused on Rimbaud syndrome in *Virtuosos of Suspense,* a novel which, much to my annoyance, continued to pursue me.

That comment about ambiguity, Cuadrelli went on, had us cornered in New York's urban maze, subject to what you might call the Indecision Regime: "The feeling that we could keep the indecision going for an unspecified length of time. It all made me think indecision could be seen as a theatrical expression of ambiguity."

From my place in the audience, I merely said to myself: Great, he's made me feel like a performer of ambiguity, and thanks to that, I know where on the stage I'll stand to give my paper tomorrow.

But of everything Cuadrelli read from "Labyrinth Doubts," what most struck me was his comment about how our meandering footsteps and the cars' sudden braking would have appeared to someone watching us from the high window of a nearby apartment. How might that observer have interpreted it all? Surely our obvious doubts would have filled them with doubts and indecisions of their own as they tried to work out why we were being so indecisive. Cuadrelli laid out the problem as follows: "I imagined someone would have been watching from a window. Had we represented an ambiguity of principle, which had the effect of generating opaque and fairly uncategorizable actions, or an ambiguity of meaning, that is, by yielding to the ambiguity that's been part of the world since the very beginning?"

This last—the ambiguity that's been part of the world since the very beginning—was, when all was said and done, what I most remembered about Cuadrelli's paper. I woke up at midnight, after a troubled sleep, wondering—now indecisive in the extreme—what ambiguity had been like in the Paleolithic caves. A question, I said to myself, that could only come from someone who, like me, had just emerged from a convoluted dream and who, moreover, had for a short time been a passionate scholar of Paleolithic caves. But no: I soon realized, to my surprise, that it wasn't *me* wondering this in my dream but my friend's son, the young mathematician Desdini, with whom I met up from time to time in the Bérgamo bar downtown.

In an attempt to better grasp the dream I'd just had, I set my mind to thinking about whether there had been time in the prehistoric caves to practice indecision with any degree of skill. If they had painted the walls of those caves, I thought, they must also have had time for ambiguity, at least for thinking about it. At any rate, I said to myself (pathologically indecisive as ever and making an enormous effort to come up with an answer), I'm sure there are marks of indecision in each one of the paintings in those caves. And then, since I was less than convinced by this line of reasoning, and bearing in mind that there was no one to catch me out, I attributed it to Desdini.

24

A survivor of hell, I continued to be simultaneously inside the Beaubourg's Bogotá and in St. Gallen, walking around with Cuadrelli. It was the day after his lecture and we were wandering through that city called Appenzell, just as, months before, we had wandered through New York: searching, indecisively, for a restaurant. After a great deal of dithering, in which our hesitation syndrome ran wild, we decided to go into Café Gschwend, at 7 Goliathgasse. We went up some narrow stairs to the dining room on the first floor. The young Swiss waitress spoke our language because, she said, she was married to a Spaniard, a die-hard supporter of Real Madrid.

After some fresh indecision—nothing out of the ordinary, just the usual for both of us—Cuadrelli decided to stick to beer rather than ordering any more food, whereas I ordered a main dish the name of which was as unintelligible as all the others: *cannegehirne*. I didn't want to ask the waitress to explain it, preferring to give Cuadrelli the impression I was a true connoisseur of the cuisine from that city and to prevent him getting the idea that I was in some way reenacting the scene from New York involving my doubts about ambiguity.

Besides, it was quite normal for me to be thinking, there in St. Gallen, about the sequence of events in New York, because several hours had gone by since Cuadrelli's paper and the word *ambiguity* had been looming ever larger between us. And also in general, throughout the whole conference, to the extent that running into another delegate in the hotel corridor could turn into a rather theatrical celebration of that phenomenon which occurs when we interpret a real-life event in two completely different ways.

We'd begun eating in silence when I came out with a reckless question, potentially provocative, and unnecessary at that. I asked him if the man walking around with him in "Labyrinth Doubts" was in fact me. Cuadrelli looked around for a toothpick and, on finding there weren't any, asked for some to be brought over. And this transaction, involving the

Real Madrid waitress, used up an entire valuable minute in which the conversation tailed off.

When we resumed it, I forgot I'd been meaning to approach the topic with caution and instead launched into a description of my trip to Montevideo in search of the room from Cortázar's "The Sealed Door." The title of that story meant nothing to Cuadrelli, and I thought he seemed surprised by my apparent interest in that door and in the potentially dreadful reality that I believed it was hiding.

I considered telling him the reason for my interest, not that I was entirely sure what it was. And since I couldn't quite put my finger on it, I decided it would be best to steer the conversation toward simpler matters, rather than getting caught up in how hard it is to explain all those completely mysterious phenomena that no one has ever properly made sense of.

Think about it, I said. There's not one writer, however much psychoanalysis they go through, who really knows why they write. Some do, Cuadrelli said, but they're idiots. I don't know, I went on, of a single writer who has managed to explain why, for example, on encountering a problem in whatever they're writing, they then find that, if they go out for a walk, the problem has been solved by the time they get home. Before, I said, it was called "inspiration," and long before that, "divine breath," but there's not a single writer who knows what's really going on there—well, aside from the really bad ones, I added. Yes, Cuadrelli said, that's true, the really bad ones stupidly explain everything they've done in great detail, which only serves to show that they're not writers at all. They think explaining the book means explaining the story within it. And the worst writers of all, I said, are the ones who say they can't explain the most interesting part of the story because that would spoil it. We both laughed. If it's a good novel, he said, there's nothing more for the author to add, nothing more to tell, or there shouldn't be, if the author has done their job properly, and the reason this is always true is that writing a novel in the first place means explaining something that happened in the writer's life or thoughts, something that demanded to be put into words and ended up giving shape to the book.

I agreed wholeheartedly. After all, I said, offering an explanation is never straightforward and is rather a hopeless, even redundant task. A little later on, we returned to the question of inspiration and what had once been called "divine breath." Yes, he said, true writers believe in nothing but this breath. Just look at Coleridge; it dictated a whole poem to him. And probably all his other work, too, I added, trying on this snide remark for size. Yes, exactly, he said. You only have to read the interviews with writers after they publish a new book, I said, to see that no one knows how to explain what they've done. Absolutely, said Cuadrelli, it's as if everyone were taking dictation from someone in the room next door. I asked him what he thought the occupant of that room was called. The Breath, he said. And he seemed quite happy with that. But I wasn't. How was I supposed to take it? I let it glide right over me. Like the faintest breath of all.

25

We'd been talking about writers as if we weren't writers ourselves, and as if not feeling like writers suited us just fine.

What put a stop to it all, inevitably, was that mention, which I took as ironic, of the "next-door room," perhaps because the allusion made us both feel like writers again, and especially me, even blocked as I was by my syndrome. It was odd because, barring that strange final stretch, the conversation had flowed nicely, though there had been that rather contrived or at the very least disconcerting twist of Cuadrelli believing in the Breath. But of course, I couldn't ask him to explain what he meant, because he'd only have said that doing so would spoil the mystery. I tried to steer him onto the topic of my fascination with doors, thresholds, and keys, and the only way I could think of was to tell him an old Chinese proverb ("The best kind of closed door is one you can leave unlocked"), which sent a flicker of disapproval across his face, either because he found my Oriental aside foolish or because he simply wasn't all that interested in doors.

Everything was turned on its head when Cuadrelli, a little tipsy by then, gave a number of signals that he was in fact entirely familiar with "The Sealed Door." And precisely because he knew the story so well, he said, he'd been wondering for a while about a detail that still baffled him from my trip to Montevideo: Why hadn't I been able to go back through the sealed door, when I'd been through it just a few hours earlier? I wish I knew that myself, I told him, but I've come to believe I got mixed up with some sort of faction of a Masonic lodge, the same one I know held numerous meetings in the hotel when it was still called the Cervantes.

Cuadrelli looked at me incredulously, doing his best not to laugh. Rather than a lodge, he said, it would have been one of those minor secret societies that exist in many parts of the world and together form what I believe is known as the Cortázar Ring, or the Cronopio Mansion, or the Crab Mansion, or something along those lines.

It's crossed my mind, too, I said right away. I only mentioned the lodge to throw you off the scent, to lure you into a confession in case you really do belong to the Cortázar Spider.

"The Cortázar Ring," he corrected me. "Or the Order of the Supreme High Cronopio, if you prefer."

"No, the Order of the Supreme High Spider," I insisted, in case an oblique reference to the main spider at hand finally led to some kind of breakthrough.

And I told him about the web of managers and staff who, as I talked about Cortázar, had begun appearing in the highly congested reception area of the Esplendor in Montevideo. But that's quite a leap, Cuadrelli said with a chuckle, because I can see the connection you draw between Cortázar worshippers and the Order of the Supreme High Spider but not what they have to do with hotels. Perhaps, I said, they're beings adrift in the world, green globes with frog heads, drawings in the margins, that whole family of animals that appeared in Cortázar's stories. They weren't animals, Cuadrelli said. They were green globes, famas, cronopios. There were no frogs, or tadpoles, or mosquitoes.

There was one on a green globe, I said, though this was nothing but hearsay and Cuadrelli quite possibly realized as much, because another flicker of disapproval crossed his face. One what? he asked. One frog, I said. It must have been the cousin of a cronopio, he said, clearly making fun of me. And what was that you said about the Order of the Supreme High Cronopio? No, Cuadrelli said, I was talking about the Order of the Lord High Frog.

I couldn't help myself, and ended up asking, in a kind of strangled shriek, if we could please go back to being (or at the very least, to talking) like writers.

"In the Order of the Lord High Frog, everyone's a writer," he said.

26

I was in Bogotá and Bogotá wasn't there, and meanwhile I was eating lunch with an increasingly worked-up Cuadrelli in St. Gallen. And then my Swiss cannelloni arrived. What a strange-looking dish, I said, taken aback. Well, it had a strange-sounding name, *cannegehirne,* Cuadrelli reminded me. Do you think it's made by a Swiss chapter of the Lord High Froggers?

Froggers? I wasn't sure that was a real word. And I didn't respond. What could I say? It was perhaps the most definitive sign yet that he belonged to that presumably Cortazarian order and couldn't resist dropping hints about it. Or it may, on the contrary, have just been a game, a way of mocking whatever concerns I might have had.

After all, during our walk before lunch, Cuadrelli had insinuated that all the ghosts I was so obviously carrying around were due to the fact that I was a professional writer who did no actual writing and that all the time I saved by not sitting at my desk I then squandered getting mixed up with spiders.

In other words, and indeed almost the very words used by Cuadrelli himself: for a writer, whether he's writing or cutting all ties with his trade, the mysterious contributions of his subconscious are *phantasmagorical,* because the subconscious tends to be in daily contact with unknown spirits, or spirits he has started to recognize, before long acquiring a seemingly supernatural force, meaning, what's more, that he grows accustomed to spectral things and is therefore perfectly capable of seeing a spider—one that's very black and very much alive—in the place of a black polo-neck sweater.

I couldn't accept that kind of speculation. And since my six *cannegehirne,* in addition to each being shaped like a human brain, had proved a thoroughly ambiguous delicacy, I changed the subject and observed that it was as if they were paying tribute to our no less ambiguous conference. Cuadrelli shot me another disapproving look, just as he had when I quoted the Chinese proverb. And before I knew it he was taking a photo of the peculiar, psychedelic dish. You'll have to send that photo to me in Barcelona, I said. And since the dish didn't look the slightest bit appetizing, I politely offered some to Cuadrelli, who immediately asked if I wanted him to turn into an amoeba. Have you ever seen a case of those brain-eating amoebas? he asked. As a matter of fact I hadn't, I said, and nor had I even known that amoebas engaged in such things.

We only started to see eye to eye again after deciding to christen that main course *cannelloni cannegehirne.* To my surprise, Cuadrelli burst out laughing, but purely, he said, because all that psychedelia was reminding him of my hometown. I didn't know what he was talking about, because Barcelona was gray and far from psychedelic. And it also, he said, reminded him of Cortázar, who had lived in my city as a very young boy. I'd had no idea about that. Apparently, aged around ten, the creator of cronopios began to be tormented by psychedelic images in the form of mosaics, which looked like lights from other worlds. When he asked his mother where all those strange visions were coming from, she told him they were reflections of Park Güell in Barcelona, where he'd been taken to play every day when he was two or three years old.

You can't seem to decide if you're finished with those, the waitress interjected sarcastically, on seeing we hadn't touched our *cannegehirne*. I was about to explain that it wasn't indecision but rather fascination and veiled disgust in the face of such cerebral fare. But in the end, since she understood Spanish, I told her it had struck me as a very strange dish, and so beautiful that I didn't want to spoil it by eating it. I understand, she said, unconvinced. And besides, I added, it's incredibly ambiguous. I think it's meant to be admired, not consumed. She said nothing and looked at me as if she no longer understood. Then she turned and walked away, just as Roy Orbison came over the speakers with "She's a Mystery to Me." And it occurred to me that the waitress, accustomed to a strictly soccer-related vocabulary, had probably stopped understanding Spanish.

27

I haven't told you this yet, said Cuadrelli, but your Montevideo episode makes me think of "Story with Mygales." Briefly puzzled, I then remembered, or thought I remembered, that title from Cortázar, although I wasn't certain Cuadrelli was talking about that story and didn't want to mention Cortázar out of the blue and come across as too obsessed. Yes, Cuadrelli said, a much later Cortázar story than "The Sealed Door," in which he returns to the topic of adjoining rooms, though in this case it's in a bungalow in Martinique rather than a hotel.

I was by no means an expert in the Argentinean writer, although lately it felt as though I was living inside his stories. And I did remember reading that "Story with Mygales," many years ago, in the magazine *Quimera,* and not really understanding it. Perhaps as a result, it had pursued me for a while, but then it stopped and I forgot all about it. One of the things I hadn't understood was what the hell mygales even were. There was no Wikipedia back then, and although I had dictionaries at home, I tended not to use them. Then I'll fill you in, Cuadrelli said. Mygales are gigantic, voracious spiders found in South America and Africa. Plenty grow to be up to ten inches across, leg span included, and they feed on small creatures, even birds. In short, they're horrific.

Nor had I understood, on my first reading of that story, some aspects of the plot, not only because I hadn't known what a mygale was but because the events were so ambiguous. When I said as much to Cuadrelli, he gave me a potted version of the story, explaining that it was about two women, the narrators, who traveled to a beach in Martinique and stayed in one wing of a bungalow divided in two. Perhaps I recalled, said Cuadrelli, how the narrators were initially bothered by the whispering of the two young women staying next door and how this then turned into curiosity about them, about the other side of the bungalow. The story came to an abrupt end as the narrators grew ever more aggressive or, in other words, underwent a mutation, a process of transformation into mygales primed to kill.

Behind this, said Cuadrelli, lay one of the first sentences of the story, which by the end could be read ironically: "We are a reciprocal marvel as neighbors, we respect each other in an almost exaggerated way."

And ahead of it, awaiting its chance, lay the ambiguous finale, open to a huge range of interpretations, although the most obvious, if anything in that story could be considered obvious, was that the narrators had regressed to a more primitive state. Primitive in the extreme, so much so that everything suggested a kind of animality: they were becoming giant spiders, six inches or more in size, killers with eight legs like meat hooks: "It's simply a matter of going around the hedge that further separates the two wings of the bungalow; the door is still closed but we know it isn't locked, that all we have to do is lift the latch. There's no light inside when we go in together . . . ."

On being reminded of this moment, when the two narrators infiltrate the other wing of the bungalow like murderous mygales, I also partly recovered the memory of that story and, above all, of its ending, which at the time I had found so difficult to make sense of and which now in fact reminded me of myself in Room 205 of the Esplendor, trying to reach Room 206 through the sealed door and finding it shut, and not only that, but with a minuscule spider newly drawn beside the keyhole . . . .

And then, piecing all this together, I finally realized that Cuadrelli had been trying for a while to explain something that should have struck me ages ago: the giant spider in Montevideo, the live spider some six inches across, could very well have been a mygale.

28

I was still in that hellish Bogotá inside the Beaubourg, standing before the two possible exits, even as I was walking around St. Gallen with Cuadrelli. I felt excited about what was being set in motion, especially because from a young age I had tried to keep up with the rapid-fire brain circuits that capture and connect distant points in space. Paris, Bogotá, Cascais, St. Gallen, Barcelona, and Montevideo were, at that moment, the brain circuit around which, as if I were my camera, I moved in the darkness like the radar on a ship, finding other realities and other ports—and other portals.

One such portal was the door to the medieval library in St. Gallen, and at that moment Cuadrelli and I, captured by my phone camera, were making our way through it, after suffering the ordeal of having to put on some vast, voluminous slippers, which Cuadrelli, rather inappropriately, compared to mygales.

It was the day after that strange lunch in Café Gschwend on Goliathgasse. And further peculiarities, though not in the form of food, awaited us in that library, none more bizarre than the experience of entering the main hall, which was dazzlingly baroque, and seeing that the fifty thousand manuscripts chosen to be displayed there shared the space with the Egyptian mummy Shep-en-Isis (Schepenese). Visitors would bump into her on turning around after examining the contents of an ancient map or feasting their eyes on the spines of old books lined up in immaculate display cases. And when they did, they got a serious fright.

Schepenese, we later found out, had been discovered in

the nineteenth century in the southern part of the mortuary temple of Hatshepsut, on the west bank of the Nile. One year later, she had been sent to Switzerland, where she became both an object of study for researchers and the most famous Egyptian mummy in the country. And I'd even say that the sight of that oddity—odd as we were ourselves sometimes, noticing only anomalous or incomprehensible things—momentarily brought us together, so much so that we had fun reciting in unison a phrase by Frédéric Dard, whom neither of us had ever read, not even by chance, and about whom all we knew was that he was the author of three hundred novels and this immortal line: "Je me suis *suissidé* en Suisse."

Everything in St. Gallen's medieval library seemed to exist at the border between reality and fiction, but it was all real, immensely real, which didn't stop me remembering that the visible was still very much a hangover of the invisible. In a way, the invisible made its presence felt most forcefully while the two of us were concentrating on the rather unpleasant sight of the mummy, and Cuadrelli surprised me by mentioning the name of a place I'd never heard of, distant and unknown: Zihuatanejo, a beach on Mexico's Pacific Coast, and some bungalows called Las Urracas, where he suspected that Cortázar had either written or had the idea for "Story with Mygales."

On hearing this, I immediately said to Cuadrelli that we should remain true to the essential idea of the game, travel to Zihuatanejo and crouch down to spy—like a pair of mygales in slippers—on our neighbors in the bungalow, whoever they were, for the sheer pleasure of staging a theatrical performance about His Lordship Ambiguity. Cuadrelli acted as though he hadn't heard, and on leaving the library, as we handed back the slippers and he came out with a few more amusing comments, I apologized for going too far.

Objectively speaking, Cuadrelli said, you have gone far, because Zihuatanejo is beyond everything; even the name sends you on a journey to remoteness itself. As he spoke, he cast a final glance at the slippers, as if they had contained the secret of that place. I asked him if, by "remoteness," he also meant the invisible. And the strange, too, Cuadrelli replied, but most of all the Other.

The Other, for Cuadrelli, was that which destroys logic and normality and disrupts the course of everyday life; it was a strong presence, he went on, in Cortázar's stories, from the very first one, "House Taken Over," where the Other is an impersonal force, something nameless that invades the house and begins occupying the space, obliging the people who live there to do so in a different way, perhaps by reconstructing it.

Yes, that's true, I said to Cuadrelli, and then tried to insinuate that the Other reappeared in "The Sealed Door." But Cuadrelli, betraying more knowledge of Cortázar's stories with every minute that passed, had by now acquired the habit of going further than me on every point. And right away he said—stumbling on the words because of how much he'd drunk—that the Other did indeed reappear in "The Sealed Door," but most of all, many years later, in the most ambiguous of Cortázar's stories, the one that he had, in fact, been talking about for hours.

"'Story with Mygales'?"

Precisely, said Cuadrelli. A story where the Other, the strange, was represented by the pair of narrators, and so too the unknown, because the reader knew everything about the life of the tourists on that that semideserted beach in Martinique with its mostly unoccupied bungalows, but eventually, in the middle of that terrifying and only very loosely sketched night, they had almost no choice but to infer . . . .

Here, he began to cough and fidget nervously, in part due to the large quantity of alcohol he had imbibed and in part, I sensed, in the hope of frightening me, not that I knew why he wanted to do that.

Once his coughing fit was over, there followed a long and suspenseful pause, after which he recovered his ability to speak and picked up where he left off, telling me that Cortázar's reader had no choice but to infer that the narrators were mygales with four lungs and fearsomely strong jaws and legs, ready to burst into that beachgoers' world so as to alter it, to reconstruct it through the oft-effective method of destroying it first—and, without a doubt, to kill.

29

Several hours later, in the lively hotel bar, I ran into Cuadrelli again. He was fresh from the shower, had clearly stopped drinking a while ago, and was so much restored that he seemed almost like somebody else, like the most serene and charming person in the world.

I made the most of this radical transformation to confess, leaving no room for ambiguity, that I'd had no idea he was such a formidable drinker. And Cuadrelli, with exquisite manners and in stark contrast to his verbal anarchy of a few hours ago, wanted to know whether he'd tired me out with his "always provisional" ideas.

I told him the truth as I saw it, namely that his long-winded half-hour spiel about the Egyptian mummy Shep-en-Isis had been rather hard work but that the rest of the time he'd been very entertaining.

"That's what my father used to say," Cuadrelli replied. "Drunks are often like clowns for respectable people, and the rabble don't deserve all that effort to entertain them."

I refused to take it personally. The main thing, I thought, is that now it's possible to talk to him. But then he withdrew into a strange silence, as if sobering up had plunged him into a powerful melancholy, a strange silence from which he emerged only now and then, always in the grip of a curious shyness, and only ever to begin sentences that had no end. Like, for example:

"Speaking of Egypt . . . ."

The typical behavior of someone who's called time on the drinking and gone from opining loudly on everything to the opposite extreme.

"Speaking of Egypt, what?"

For a few seconds I heard him muttering in a way that suggested the barely audible vibrations of a man running through what he was going to say, though I then saw that he'd known perfectly well all along.

"Speaking of Egypt, I've been pondering your Montevideo episode, and I think I have something to tell you about the symbolic mygale that crossed your path."

According to Cuadrelli, the Montevidean mygale on the red suitcase was in no way a chance event, much as it might have seemed like one or could in theory have been one. Most likely, he said, that little pencil drawing of the spider in the middle of the sealed door was left there as an Egyptian-style visual puzzle.

What was he talking about? The kind of visual puzzle, he

went on, that was used, in centuries gone by, and especially in Egypt, by poets and theologians in the service of the pharaohs. I'd already considered that, I said, but didn't want to suggest it for fear of sounding even more paranoid. Well, in that case you'll know, he said, that the poets and theologians of ancient Egypt thought it impious to use ordinary script to convey the mysteries of knowledge to the lay population.

I knew a bit, but not much, I confessed. Well, you see, if they thought something was worth knowing, they depicted it using the figures of various animals and objects, so that it didn't reach the general public, but only those whose understanding of the symbols meant they were in on the secret.

When I heard the word *secret,* I began to think about the question I most wanted to ask him, a question that in fact fit very well with my Cortazarian paranoia, which had only increased in recent hours, since, among other transformations, I had suddenly grown wise to something incredible that had passed me by for too long: the surname Cuadrelli belonged to a famous character from *Hopscotch.* If I wasn't mistaken, the Cuadrelli in Cortázar's book was an elderly writer convinced that the novel as a genre had been changing its rules over time and had the advantage of not being obliged to conform to any pattern.

A coincidence, no doubt, but my life was filling up with coincidences. And as if that weren't enough, I had just remembered—though I was deceiving myself—that the Cuadrelli in *Hopscotch* was the "critical conscience of the narrator," that is, of Cortázar himself. And there was another coincidence that now seemed clear to me and that I wanted to explore: the fake spider that separated my balcony in Cascais from that of Jean-Pierre Léaud.

After giving him a brief rundown of my night in Cascais, I asked Cuadrelli what he made of that coincidence, of my encountering a fake spider before the live mygale and the spider drawing in Montevideo. It was a leading question, intended to move us onto a discussion of the very sizable coincidence of him being called Cuadrelli, and therefore sharing a name with that character from *Hopscotch*.

The Cascais spider, he said, is in no way suspicious; it was merely a hypermodern affectation on the part of that hotel. Only that, Cuadrelli? Well, if you want to split hairs, or hairy spiders, you may like to recall that Léaud appeared in Godard's *Weekend,* which was based on a Cortázar story. Yes, I know, I said, it was based on "The Southern Thruway." Exactly, he said, but that leads to a dead end, wouldn't you say? Well, I said, I think it all leads to Cortázar. Or does it? Cuadrelli asked. Perhaps it only leads us to a writer who turned out to be more frog than prince, but I bet you couldn't think of a single one who didn't turn out to be a frog in the end.

I felt as if he'd handed me the answer on a plate. I wouldn't be so sure, I said. I can think of Cuadrelli, for example, the character from *Hopscotch*. And right away, accompanied by a scandalized expression, came his clincher of a question:

"Don't you mean Morelli?"

I wanted the ground to swallow me up. No Cuadrelli had ever been the "critical conscience" of the narrator of *Hopscotch*. There wasn't a single Cuadrelli in the book. I could permit myself a few mistakes about Cortázar's work, since I'd never claimed to be a connoisseur, but confusing a name like Cuadrelli with Morelli made me look utterly ridiculous. And indeed, he was staring at me as if I were the one who'd had a few too many that day.

I've just remembered, Cuadrelli said, I need to say good night to a small frog in the pond. And with that excuse, a far-fetched one by any standards, he disappeared from the bar and, hurrying for no discernible reason, jogged down some steps into the hotel garden, so as to heighten, presumably for my benefit, the unmistakable impression that he was escaping.

Not long after that, I went and stood by the big window overlooking the garden below; I wanted to see if Cuadrelli had really gone out there. And he very much had: not only that, but he'd fallen into the pond and was being helped back onto dry land. Someone who'd just joined me by the window, Samuel Branner, a world authority on ambiguity, observed: There's nothing like not being the slightest bit drunk to make it seem as if you are.

30

That evening, I met up with Yvette Sánchez and mentioned the mistake I'd made two hours before, when I'd confused Cuadrelli with Morelli. In her view, that confusion was simply a sign that we were surrendering to the ambiguity that's been present in the world from the very beginning. You don't say, I replied. Yes, Yvette went on, everything doesn't lead to Cortázar, as you said to Cuadrelli, but to ambiguity. It's all thanks to our conference . . . . I didn't want to contradict that verdict, which at any rate seemed hard to argue with. And after her observation, we went to have dinner, as planned, in a quiet restaurant on Marktgasse, the narrow street that is home to St. Gallen's market.

We were joined at dinner by the parish priest from a nearby town, not the one who had seemed so revered by his parishioners and with whom I'd argued a great deal on my last trip to Appenzell, but the one who had waved to us from the doorway of the St. Laurenzen church in Straubenzell: a young man nearly six and a half feet tall, dressed from head to toe in black, and with huge feet that at first seemed to be dancing on the spot, as if they were looking for something on the ground, or perhaps wanting to sweep it. At the same time, in a curious contrast, he was very slow in his speech. And almost clumsy, as well, especially when he tried to convince me that he knew all about my country, choosing to do so by praising the olive oil from the province of Jaén, among a host of other things. Endless rhapsodizing about that oil, which he very lazily expected Yvette to translate for me. Because even though that priest knew some Spanish, he stubbornly delivered his monologue in German and I didn't understand a thing, aside from the fact that he seemed very rude.

After spending longer than acceptable on a monologue that seemed formulated to include various instances of the word *Jaén,* and therefore to give him several opportunities to hone his pronunciation, that gigantic, exhausting young man—who at times I thought might have designed the slippers in the medieval library—fell silent while Yvette jumped in to explain to me that Cortázar's mygales—this was the renowned professor of Hispano-American literature in her talking—had many precedents in the Argentinean writer's work: the famous cockroaches in his story "Circe," but also countless other allusions to insects and arthropods, not to mention, she said, the analogy in "The Menades" between cockroaches and musical instruments, or indeed the analogy of the motorcycle and the insect in "The Night Face Up," etc.

In all those stories—though I'd only read some of Cortázar's most famous works, and not the texts Yvette was mentioning—the author of *Hopscotch* laid out the fragility of our condition as civilized beings living lives of modernity and progress and showed how easy it would really be to regress to more primitive stages of development.

This last phrase must have lodged in my brain, because if there's one detail from that night I won't forget in a hurry, it's how, even as Yvette was educating me about the world of insect appearances in Cortázar's literary universe, I felt I was watching just such a strong animal component take over the young cleric's body—watching, that is, a bestial element fight to overcome his human side, so much so that he was about to turn into a strange cross between a sheep and a giraffe.

A bizarre occurrence, which, rather than leaving me worried about what might be happening to this messenger of God, made me reflect on how little I knew about Cortázar's notable ability to transform his human characters into animals, something which, depending on your point of view, could be a legacy from the Paleolithic age, when the categories we deal in today—woman, man, horse, tree, door—can shift and change.

After dinner, I returned to the hotel on Poststrasse, accompanied by Yvette, who wanted to leave me at the entrance to the Walhalla, where she knew everyone, which in itself was a sight to behold. Yvette took advantage of my guard being down to scold me for something I'd been afraid she'd disapprove of in the moment: all my rather pointed comments to her good friend about the Himalayas, which I could now barely remember. His height is none of your business, she even said.

Just before we parted ways for the night, she sent me a picture from her phone that she'd found online and had saved, she said, with me in mind. It was a short letter from Elena Poniatowska to Cortázar and had seemed right up my street, she went on, because I was in such determined pursuit of the author of "The Pursuer." I protested: I didn't think I was pursuing Cortázar in the slightest; on the contrary, at least since I'd returned from Montevideo, it seemed more as if his shadow was pursuing *me*. But Yvette cut me off with a few more reproaches, one more unexpected than the rest, because it was about how I'd been looking disdainfully at the young priest all evening. It's one thing to think from time to time that someone's mutating into a cross between a giraffe and a large mole, she said, but it's quite another to tell them. Just be glad I decided not to translate that part. Yes, he's tall, but he's the same height as Julio Cortázar, six foot three, so I think we can forgive him, don't you?

31

I remained hypnotized in my Beaubourg hell and at the same time—not for nothing was I facing the two doors—I was opening the door to Room 27 in my hotel in St. Gallen. It was gratifying to have been assigned that room, what with the number 27's proven reputation, its status as a magical number linked to philanthropy and selfless work for the good of other people.

I looked in my work folder for the speech about ambiguity I'd written before being brought up short by the fragment "Paris." A lecture on the ancestral ambiguity of the world, so powerfully enhanced in recent times by quantum theory, which questions even what we see and what we understand as reality.

But "work folder" is really just a manner of speaking, because for some time I hadn't produced any work at all, and that lecture had been finished long before I fell into the pit of not writing. In fact, I'd been counting on dozing off while making my pointless revisions to that speech, which I hadn't even planned to tweak in case I immediately stopped being a victim of my own syndrome, and this left me feeling oddly bereft in a way I couldn't quite pin down, though at the same time I found it rather exciting, given how freeing it was to go around in the world without my literary baggage.

I'd been counting on falling asleep during those pointless revisions, and I did. Like a log, as they say. But I woke up suddenly a few hours later, when a murmur of voices reached my ears from the room next door: a conversation between three or four people, maybe more, a hushed exchange, placid and anodyne, the sort that might take place in a bungalow in Martinique, a hum of pure routine, though coming from the very center of the deep dark night.

It was a shock, needless to say, when I recognized Cuadrelli's voice among them, with its unmistakable Buenos Aires accent, filtered through his spells in Boston and New York. The sound of his voice, let alone his presence in the room next door to mine—something it was strange for him not to have mentioned earlier—made me uneasy, and grew all the more bewildering when the whispers, after fading away, then began to increase in volume and eventually burst into the opening notes of a song that the group was, to all appearances, intending to sing as a trio.

I threw on my clothes, stormed into the corridor, and saw they'd left the door to the room ajar. A trap, I thought, before pushing at the door with ambiguous caution, since when it came down to it, given the circumstances, *I* was more likely to scare *them* witless. And then all of a sudden I was faced with an absurd panorama that frankly seemed designed for my benefit: Cuadrelli, sober as a judge, sitting on the bed and slowly untying a red necktie, with a small frog that was clearly dead, stone dead, resting on his right leg. A corpse, yet in no way motionless, because the frog was hanging from a thread that had presumably been sewn into the left pocket of Cuadrelli's jacket. I asked Cuadrelli, with steely calm, if this was the frog from the pond, and if there was any particular reason why he was using it as a pocket watch.

The correct answer would have been: Yes, it's the frog that was caught in the hotel pond. But Cuadrelli clearly had no intention of saying much, or anything at all, and nor had he shown any signs of being pleased to see me; in fact, he barely seemed to recognize me, though I couldn't think of any plausible reason why not.

I was told by one of the twins who were with him that the three of them were getting ready to sing "Senza un perché." The twins were two corpulent middle-aged women with bodies like Amazons whom I'd seen around at the "Ambiguity Conference." Two Valkyries who were in no way Germanic but rather had an indisputably Italian air. And a-one, and a-two, and a-three, the pair chanted in unison. Then, without further ado, they launched into the chorus:

E tutta la vita
Gira infinita senza un perché
E tutto viene dal niente
E niente rimane senza de te.

You know, the twins said to me afterward in Italian, there isn't a chorus more perfect than the one we just sang, because it encapsulates everything that happens in this world, and you have to realize that no one under the Sun has suffered the way we have. I can't tell you how sorry I am, I stammered, in the politest tone I could muster. Well, believe you me, she went on, life has dealt us a bad hand. And death, too, quipped the blonder twin, blonder and plainly the prime candidate for being the more wicked of the two.

I looked at Cuadrelli, trying to convey once and for all my total astonishment at the scene playing out before my eyes. I was going to ask him, rather tongue in cheek, whether the frog was an homage to the Montevidean mygale, but then decided against venturing into such dangerous terrain. What was more, ever since my confusion between Cuadrelli and Morelli, I felt less sure of myself around him, sensing that he viewed me with distrust, and more than a little condescension.

I was going to ask him why he hadn't mentioned he was in the room next door to mine, but before I could, Cuadrelli, always ahead of the game, had pulled a deeply strange face, which made him look completely different than usual. His expression had changed from one second to the next and even become quite hair-raising, for there's no better adjective than *hair-raising* to describe the feeling of fright when a person we think we know suddenly reveals an unexpected side of themselves that we had no idea about at all.

He looked like *someone else*. And I thought about what Sergio Chejfec had written in *Elevator Theory,* about a person who ended up thinking they had turned into someone else, though not in the traditional way, because, as Chejfec said, for him "being someone else" was less to do with having a new personality than with entering a new world, a world where reality and all the people in it had lost or discarded their memory and allowed him in as an unknown member, a new arrival.

32

Rather than continuing to stare into Cuadrelli's eyes— an experience that took me back to the time I gazed uninterruptedly into the darkness and everything began to feel rather sinister, even terrifying—I stared affectionately at the frog. At first, though I was seeing it from a distance, the silent frog reminded me of an obviously much smaller version of the Montevidean mygale. With the caveat that there, in St. Gallen, that filipendulous frog had a lethal tendency to take flight even in death, to take flight and then return to its new owner's leg, that human leg to which it had been condemned and which had clearly become its home and tomb that night.

Albeit without looking at him, I said to Cuadrelli that the frog, however deceased, would in time grow up and emigrate to the Caribbean, to Martinique, and leave him on his own, just as all children leave their parents; that it would sally forth from his leg and sign up to the Order of the Supreme Frogs. And Cuadrelli simply gave me a terrible smile—chilly, frosty, utterly glacial.

I'd better get out of here, I thought. But not without satisfying my frustrated curiosity from a minute before. And so, treacherously, I asked why he hadn't told me we were in neighboring rooms. He didn't even answer, though he seemed to want to convey that it was news to him as well.

Still, no response was forthcoming; he had fallen silent, in perfect harmony with the lifeless frog. I asked him then if he was perhaps staging a parody of what had happened to me in the Montevideo hotel. And if it was a parody, I said, then congratulations were in order, because it had been very well put together, and moreover I was grateful that, instead of a red suitcase and a gigantic live insect, he had involved his musical friends.

Cuadrelli's face remained impassive, and again there was no response.

I thought: the world is full of intelligent people who, when you throw them a ball, instead of catching it and returning it, keep hold of it and then launch into a monologue and outwardly spurn the conversation. But there was no reason why this should always be the case with an excellent conversationalist such as Cuadrelli. Still, he seemed troubled by something that was clearly lost on me. I could tell he wasn't under the influence of alcohol—I'm an expert in that area. Even so, I decided to ask the twins if he'd hit the bottle again. No, not at all, he's just like this at night, said one twin. He's drunk nothing but the moonlight, said the other.

In an attempt to get through to Cuadrelli however I could, I asked him if the frog was a symbol of something, one of those Egyptian signs he'd been telling me about some hours before in the hotel bar. He remained silent. I asked again, but deliberately using a phrase constructed in a language that would free him from the one we normally used, and which perhaps he had grown tired of. But not even this ruse could draw him from his silence, the silence of a tomb, of the tomb of a frog, and his expression didn't change one jot. And I saw that the little toad—because just then it looked to me more like a toad than a frog—came together with the motionless Egyptian statue that was Cuadrelli to form a great funereal monument, in marked contrast to the vivacious twins, who kept shouting at me, asking if they could sing the whole of "Senza un perché." And why, I wondered, why, in heaven's name, were they so desperate to make it through "Senza un perché" at this time of night?

33

Dear Julio:
Please accept this little book from woman no. 16753134758293002 who's writing you letter XYZ no. 32/V/374742, this trifling little book, not so you'll read it, but just so you'll see that p. 171 shares your interest in the green ray, which I was delighted to learn about after reading your article. I wish you a Merry Christmas and a wonderful New Year 1980. Lots of love and admiration *and other spiders,* Elena.

34

I'd better get out of here quick-smart, I said to myself, out of this hellish Bogotá and this ghastly St. Gallen room with its singing quartet.

Like someone coming back from a long journey to the center of an unclassifiable anomaly, I returned to my room in that hotel on Poststrasse and soon managed to doze off again, although from time to time I opened my eyes in my sleep and saw the ghost from my Barcelona guest room beginning to take shape. The ghost, as it materialized, revealed a great fondness for moving closets around; it seemed even sillier than the ghost from that brilliant Dickens story, which at least tried to warm itself up by using the wood from his closet to make a fire. And in one of those fleeting awakenings I again heard the disquieting hum of voices from the Italo-Argentine choir and their associated frog. But by now, it seemed, the murmurs were fading, the voices very much on the wane. I felt calmer than before. The other noises, the nocturnal sounds outside the hotel, did admittedly grow gradually louder, reflecting the rhythm of the things and the stars. And, for a moment, I even managed a laugh as I told myself that, if the Valkyries and Cuadrelli with his little dead toad could see me on the other side of the wall, they'd be struck dumb by the realization that I'd turned into a mygale in the darkness and was stalking them all, dressed to kill and comforted by the proximity of that deadly quartet, which meant food and useful company, and living or dead flesh, because you had to wonder what would become of the nights in this world if beasts were left with no humans or occasional surplus frogs in adjoining rooms.

Hours later, for one extraordinary moment just before dawn, I fantasized about waking with the sun, with a guava juice and a steaming cup of coffee, and the long, strange Swiss night behind me with its bursts of tropical rain and sudden downpours that always stopped as abruptly as they'd started, in a way that seemed almost apologetic.

But very soon, as dawn was breaking, reality gave the lie to the American night, the imagined night, the red-headed night, the Martinican night, the night of the iguana and the guava, the night of the singing quartet in the room next door. I learned from the night porter, whom I called on the hotel phone because I'd noticed he was a friend of Yvette's and spoke good French, that the occupants of number 28 had left the room just a few minutes ago. That rather threw me, because I'd been thinking of waking them up and disturbing their undeserved rest. But most disconcerting of all was that I then lost track of Cuadrelli for the rest of the day. Because not only did he not show his face at my lecture, he was also absent from the delegate lunch. Only as it was getting dark did I spot him in the distance, but precisely when it was too late for everything, because I was in the red BMW convertible that Yvette had borrowed to take me to the Frankfurt airport, where my return flight awaited me.

Following what Cuadrelli had told me about groups and clubs devoted to Cortázar as a writer of short stories, Yvette was now saying that she had indeed heard about such goings-on, and that she knew he'd had no shortage of followers and that some of them organized themselves into little secret societies, occasionally carrying out highly entertaining pranks, such as replacing a bust of Victor Hugo in Paris with one of Cortázar and managing to do it in just three hours, when the state had taken three days to put it back.

She was telling me these things when we saw Cuadrelli in good company, striding very athletically along the side of the road. We almost clipped him on our way past. The problem was that we were in a hurry to get to the airport on time and couldn't easily pull over in Yvette's sports car because we were driving at a considerable speed, downhill, on Rosenbergstrasse.

Look, she said, there's your friend, the most ambiguous of them all. And that comment stayed with me, because I was beginning to think the same. Cuadrelli was like the very incarnation of ambiguity, that element so fundamental, so indispensable to anyone wanting to understand one of the main features of this world, and indeed of what lay beyond it, as I'd said in my lecture, since quantum theory even cast doubt over what we saw and understood as reality.

You don't need to tell me, I said to Yvette. I'm not sure if you're aware, but Cuadrelli heads up a vast team of people who work day and night on texts whose sole objective—and here I paused for a couple of seconds, unsure whether to say this or keep it to myself—is to discredit that trite catchphrase of Bartleby's, the famous "I would prefer not to."

35

Yvette laughed, though she didn't have the faintest idea what I was getting at with that statement, and indeed neither did I, since I'd made it up on the spot. And as she laughed—Yvette has always laughed a lot, a sign of an intellect that knows how to have fun—I went on begging her to stop the car so I could bid farewell to Cuadrelli. Turn back for a second, I want to say goodbye, I kept repeating, there's something I need him to explain. But we were barreling along the highway that led to Rosenberg and it wasn't a good moment to slam on the brakes. I did have time to see Cuadrelli, holding a rudimentary walking stick and transformed into a happy-go-lucky and competent-seeming mountaineer, merrily making his way down the hill with some young women who were just as athletic as he was, and also the two ineffable Valkyries who, despite their respective physiques, at no point ended up lagging behind that energetic group.

And Cuadrelli was laughing, laughing even harder than Yvette at the wheel, which was really saying something. At this point Yvette finally noticed quite how desperate I was to say goodbye, and so, with the requisite caution, she turned the BMW around and made the brief, swift ascent up the few rolling inclines that separated us from the sporty-looking set.

Cuadrelli was just as surprised as you'd expect to find us suddenly in front of him. At the same time, however, he didn't pass up the opportunity to display his upbeat, open side, his jolly postmeridian persona, though the mask slipped when that icy smile from the night before seeped into his expression, the smile that gave him away and made him unrecognizable to everyone.

Even so, this time I looked him straight in the eye and told him I was flying back to Barcelona but that first I wanted to know if he could give me any clue as to his behavior during the turbulent events of the previous night. He stared at me open-mouthed, as if he didn't know what I was talking about. And he succeeded in making me nervous, so I cut to the chase and asked him about the frog and the "Senza un perché."

"Volare," we heard him say.

And that was it, from then on he didn't say another word, only that *Volare,* which seemed more of a comment than a response. Yvette asked me what exactly he'd said but also reminded me that we had to get a move on, and seconds later she was back at the wheel of her borrowed convertible and we were making for the airport once more, when the door leading out of my Colombian hell—the visible door, the one I couldn't unlock and walk through—opened from the other side and, in a thoroughly unexpected twist, in burst Madeleine Moore and Dominique González-Foerster, two experts—I remembered right away—in artistic actions they called "appearances."

"You are in the Beaubourg," they said in unison.

I didn't mind them parodying that "You are in Bogotá," but I did mind them obstructing, with their sudden entrance, the view of my descent in Yvette's convertible down the Rosenberg highway. And I minded when they went on to inquire if I'd been shut in that room for very long. Among the questions I felt I had to ask them was whether they'd had any trouble getting in through that door which I'd tried in vain to get out of. And another was why on earth they seemed so ecstatically happy to have turned up in my hell.

The two of them appeared to be quite at home, which wasn't surprising, because they were; the Splendide *was them.* Amused and triumphant, they asked why I kept on pointing my phone camera at them. I soon saw that, if I explained in a reasonable way, they wouldn't understand at first what they were blocking, what they were covering up. So I opted for the direct approach. I asked if they were aware of the incredible discovery I'd made while using the night mode on my phone. Not remotely, said Moore, seeming very uninterested. A secret door, I said, right beside the one you just used to get into my hell. On hearing this, Moore immediately smiled at Dominique, as if to say: There, what did I tell you, he likes looking for things no one can see.

Everything I tried to explain to them about the invisible door fell on deaf ears. What was more, I had to listen to a sermon from Moore, a ticking-off that began with another phrase I also won't forget in a hurry:

"It's as if you were always in Montevideo."

That didn't sound so bad. Montevideo was a city, but it was also a state of mind, a way of living in peace far removed from the convulsive center of the world, an ancient rhythm beaten out with bare feet.

After her pronouncement, Moore began to tell me off for being, she said, overly obsessed with adjoining rooms, and also with rooms with two doors. You're the kind of person, she went on, who seems to see in their dreams a second apartment where we're all going to sleep, leaving our own homes behind. And then, barely pausing for breath, she announced that in a week's time Room 19 would be connected to a door number 20, behind which would be the "desired" adjoining room that I would no doubt, she said, be very keen to visit. I'd rather see it now, I said. That won't be possible, Dominique interrupted, but we hope you'll come back and take a look; we haven't built it yet.

Again I mentioned the new, secret door I'd just filmed, which could be seen perfectly not only by means of my phone but also in existing footage, which I could show them to prove I wasn't making it up. Besides, I said, they'd do well to take a look because they were on the cusp of seeing something potentially life-changing. Listen, the merciless Moore intervened, it's possible I even believe you, though I'm pretty sure what you've seen is the door that will be here next week, and which you might as well know you'll be able to open with your key, just as today you couldn't because the adjoining room isn't there yet.

I asked her how she thought I was able see the door she'd just told me wasn't there. By imagining you have a camera that can see the future, Moore replied. And then she added: I believe in the power of the mind, in its inner logic. By this, she clarified, she meant the power we all have to construct unprecedented backstories based on any old detail. But my new door, I protested, isn't an unprecedented backstory. And I brought up Ariel Luppino, who said there's an outer logic and an inner logic, but the inner logic doesn't get on with the outer. And then, without seeing it coming, of course, I became trapped by those words of Luppino's, because Moore jumped in and asked why I was talking about inner logic when I'd already told her I didn't believe in inner worlds.

I was wondering how to emerge from this gracefully when Dominique came to my aid, batting away the question and saying there was also the logic of the enigma, which was the most interesting of all. I've not come across that one, Moore said.

And for some reason, though I've never known why, at that moment the "tropicalization," the copious and persistent rain that was Moore's watermark and had, for a long time before that, been Dominique's, came to a sudden stop.

36

Look, said Moore, given your infuriating fascination with that Abyssinian poet, be he dead or alive, I wanted you to know what it really means to spend "a season in Hell." That's why I brought you to Bogotá. I knew you'd had an awful time there and that it would therefore be a good place for you to hear, endlessly, the most exalted things you've ever written. And listen, she went on, I also wanted you to see quite clearly what the masculine version of Virginia Woolf's "room of one's own" is usually like, and that's why I talked to you about the "only room" in a hotel, when really I was thinking about that "room of one's own," so hellish for men, where they hear recordings of their "immortal pages" and rue the day they wrote such nonsense instead of learning how to work alongside feminine literature, or if not quite that, then at least literature written by women.

And all for your own good, Moore continued, because I'm sure that having now briefly sampled your "hell of one's own," you'll start writing again, embarking this time upon a new phase, with a new style, on the other side of a new door. Bogotá might have helped you with that as well.

I felt a wave of uncontrollable resentment rush through me. A new door never helped anyone write a great new page, I said, in the voice of someone deeply aggrieved. Well, I guarantee you that this time it will. You just wait, she said. And as I heard those words, I couldn't help thinking about the new door that was still there on my phone, thrumming with future, according to Moore.

I was about to tell her that all I'd achieved in her Bogotá was feeling more uncomfortable than usual, perhaps as uncomfortable as the day when, on the terrace of Les Deux Magots, I'd silently uncovered several flaws in *La concession française*. But I stopped myself. Remembering the flaws was enough to satisfy my resentment: the book's style, for example, which would have been faultless were it not for

Moore's penchant for blank spaces and, above all, that obsession with parentheses, which invited the label *pathetic parenthetic*. And on top of that, there was what we might call the bedrock of her thinking, which could easily be reduced to clichés, inevitable in any intelligent person, but clichés nonetheless: the evil of mankind; death as a scandal; meaningless life versus meaningful suicide; the instability, creativity, and folly that will always afflict us . . . .

But I thought it best to exercise caution and avoid bringing up any of those antagonistic opinions I'd had about her book.

And now, if you don't mind, I said, I'm going to continue my journey down the Rosenberg highway.

37

The next day, I left Colombia, I left St. Gallen, I left Rosenberg, I left Frankfurt, I left the Littré, I left Paris, and I even left myself forgotten in some shadowy region of my undeserved hell, and went to Orly to catch a flight to Barcelona, thinking I'd be back a week later to see what lay in store for me in the adjoining room. With friends like these . . . I thought darkly, now and again. But even so, I wanted to go back, to find out what would be in the adjoining room that Moore was going to build me. Sometimes I felt I adored Moore. I adored her, but only when I believed that the whole thing, unpleasant as it was, had been her way of helping me out, of bringing me face-to-face with the new door.

On the night of Friday, November 13, 2015, three days before I was due to return to Paris and discover what kind of adjoining room to hell Moore had made me—I was fully expecting to find a kind of purgatory this time, and a poet called Statius who would lead me to a celestial garden, where I might perhaps be able to breathe—the jihadist attacks took place in that city, killing a hundred and thirty people and wounding four hundred more. There were shootings on the terraces of five bars and restaurants, close-range killings, and taking of hostages in the Bataclan theater, as well as explosions around the Stade de France soccer ground and at another restaurant near the Place de la Nation.

Those attacks far exceeded the tame notions of terror that had been taking shape within me since Montevideo, and I felt quite overwhelmed by what had happened, among other things because Paris, to me, was sacred ground. For a few minutes, I couldn't move or react to anything that was happening around me. Shutting my eyes, I gave way to a strange inability to imagine anything. Try as I might to think about the contents of the room in my apartment where I was at the time—the guest room, no less, where I'd had a television installed for watching movies and soccer games, and perhaps also in the hope of driving out the ghost—I couldn't envisage a thing. I opened my eyes and looked for a long time at the blank television screen and the curtain covering the window overlooking an inner courtyard. I tried to fix those two images in my mind, but the moment my eyes closed I found it impossible to visualize either the television or the curtain. When I finally opened them again and found I'd recovered the ability to move, I went outside and, once in the street, made my way to a nearby cinema.

I took in a movie described as a *masterpiece* but found it so intensely annoying that I actually took in as little of it as possible. I did, however, laugh out loud five times, at completely inappropriate moments. Then I shut my eyes, giving up on the movie, and only opened them again to go outside. And, as I made my way down the Vía Augusta, after several moments of doubt I made up my mind to steer clear of Paris for a while, because I could sense that the city had been changed overnight, and if I went now I'd taste nothing but fear in the air. I'd feel sheer terror at sitting outside one of the bars I so loved, knowing that doing so, from then on, might mean risking my life. And so convinced was I that, much to my regret, but without any doubt in my mind, I gave up on that second visit to the Splendide and thought I'd rather not leave Barcelona for some time.

Once I'd made that firm decision—so unusual for someone like me, who made very few decisions of any kind—I planned to send my Unica key, which Madeleine had promised would also open the door at the far end of the room, to someone else, so that they could go to the Beaubourg in secret and enter the room connected to number 19, and then, on their return, tell me what they had found. And although, in a monumental error, the first envoy I thought of was Navarro Falcón, I soon rejected that dreadful, appalling idea, because if that famously slapdash Barcelona character—whom people called Never-Mind Falcón—stood out for anything, it was his pathetic tendency to bump into every door he walked through, and not only that, but he was also particularly inept at describing what he saw, including anything he might see of an ordinary door, let alone if someone had drawn, for example, a fifteen-legged spider on it, along with a Swiss frog and a chameleon. Navarro Falcón would have no hope of communicating details like these, and yet he was the only person who, on hearing that I'd received the key to the annex to that room of my own in the Beaubourg, asked if he could borrow it, so as, he said, to write "an article about the event," and to be honest, I still think that if he hadn't used the alarming word *event,* I would perhaps have handed over the key. But that dreadful word made it completely impossible. And after pondering the matter and ruling out some other friends who would surely have been able to help, I decided to message Moore on WhatsApp and, after describing my extreme phobia of sitting on a Parisian terrace at any point within at least the next two or three months, asked her outright if she could tell me what there was to see in the room next to my hell.

Moore must have understood that the terraces weren't a good excuse not to go to Paris. And she was extremely laconic in her first response: "What will you see in there? Just a man who wants to *raise himself up.*" She was laconic, but that message, though I had no way of knowing at the time, in fact contained *everything,* while the next message—her response to my request for more information—seemed more eloquent but was merely a complement to the first: "Lately you've become a writer to whom things really happen. Let's hope you understand your destiny, the destiny of a man who ought now to be wanting to *raise himself up,* to be reborn, to be again. I'll say it one more time: *to raise himself up.* Your destiny—the key to the new door—is in your hands."

Paris

1

In late November I traveled to Paris to see the room next door to that room of my own, which I sometimes referred to as "my hell." I planned to make it a day trip, rather than staying the night in the city. I didn't tell Moore I'd be in the Beaubourg, preferring to go incognito, without seeing anyone, get on with my business and not hang around, just visit that annex to the hell that my genius friend had created for me, according to her with my salvation in mind, though no one had asked her for that kind of help.

In any case, I wanted to compare the door to the annex with the invisible one that I'd filmed. Afterward, my curiosity sated, I would go home and move on. I took such an early flight to Paris that I even had to wait outside the Beaubourg for it to open to the public. Next came an exhaustive security search, all the more rigorous because of my potentially suspicious gym bag. And then at last I reached the door to the only room in the Hotel Splendide, number 19, and unlocked it with no trouble using my Unica key, as I had done the week before.

To avoid the tiresome *foehn,* that Bavarian fog, I crossed the treacherous real room at top speed and armed with a flashlight. That brief, unstoppable advance toward the door at the far end felt like the theatrical representation of some verses by the still very modern Herrera y Reissig, the Montevidean poet for whom spectral reality passed "through the *tragic and murky magic lantern* of my spectral reason."

In other words, I treated hell as no more than a stopover and went straight to the door at the far end, which, unlike the week before, was marked with the number 20. More surprising than this, however, was the fact it was a new door, perhaps the same one I'd seen days before with the help of "activate night mode."

This new door had in fact now become the visible door, because the other one, the one that had been visible the previous week, had disappeared, reminding me of the missing door in Montevideo. Of course, a certain curiosity made me want to use the night mode on my camera to see *what else was there*. And yet I restrained myself, as if I didn't have time for fun and games as I took my leave of hell. The sooner I got into the annex to that room of my own, the better. This time, my Unica key did indeed unlock the door to Room 20 and, for a moment, before finding the light switch, I couldn't see a thing, or rather, on shining my flashlight into the very eyes of that darkness, I thought I made out a man from another century—I'd already seen him, under other circumstances, in my dream from the previous night—sipping on the white liquid that fills spiders' abdomens and claiming it was a delicacy, with an exquisitely subtle nutty taste.

The vision vanished as soon as the light came on, and I saw I was looking at a room just bright enough that I no longer needed my magic lantern, otherwise known as my flashlight. In the room were a television screen and a walnut chair with an upholstered seat. It didn't take me long to figure out how to work the video player, by pressing the red button of an old remote control that was on that only chair. I pressed the button and there appeared a scene from a documentary set in a hospital in Paris. Through the half-open door, the camera entered the room of someone called Duvert, a thirty-two-year-old man with a serious spinal injury caused by an AK-47 bullet during the attack on the Bataclan theater. In that room, a voiceover told me, the survivor was *working to stay alive.* He had begun to regain some movement in his body and was trying to sit up, to literally *raise himself up,* to be again.

At the end of that long scene, a second voiceover, this time from none other than Madeleine Moore, came on. She couldn't stop thinking, she said, about the refugees from the war in Syria who, after risking their lives, arrived on an island in the Mediterranean and slowly began to stand up, to *raise themselves up,* and to feel, like that man in the hospital bed, that they were being again, that is, that they were coming back to life, being *born again,* an expression that might sound like a cliché to some, but not to anyone who's been through such an extreme experience.

In a way, I thought, that scene in the hospital spoke of how people were adapting to the new reality that was already upon us, even if we didn't seem to be entirely aware of it. And yet here it was, and the outlook was terrifying, especially if you happened to be making your way toward a door at the far end of an annex to an only room and were planning to open it with the Unica key.

That door wasn't numbered like the other two, and so,

suspecting my key wouldn't work in the lock, I decided not to try it. I also turned off the night mode on my phone camera because I was worried that, behind that door and after the chaos of the terror attacks, all I would find, following the logic of succession, was a row of doors forming a corridor of death that would most likely lead to the greatest possible horror: an encounter with the authentically real, that unknown dimension which, as my father used to say, should we find ourselves before it, would be so far beyond the realms of understanding or possibility that we would faint there and then, crash into a door or wall that would appear out of nowhere, and hit the floor in a state of shock.

And so, standing facing the door at the far end of Room 20, I almost celebrated the reduction of my life to a single, sole room, with a corresponding room next door. It was enough. I didn't want to go any farther. I didn't want a room next door to the room next door.

I'd just made this decision when I took a penultimate, brief but incisive look at the unnumbered door, which, depending on your point of view, bore a certain resemblance to the sealed door. And I told myself I'd had enough, because before me was a spiraling series of doors that could only lead to horror and eventual annihilation. And yet I had fun imagining I was looking into the darkness that I sensed behind that numberless door. And my gaze—which I tried, as far as possible, to make work like my camera with its infrared night vision—could not have been any longer or deeper or more natural or less digital, and it lasted an extraordinarily long time, until, in the end, I was left feeling like a survivor trying to get up, to literally *raise himself up,* to be again.

2

Many years, sorry, *days* later—and not that many, actually, more like five—I was sitting calmly at home in Barcelona observing everything with the same "basement perspective" with which I tended to see things in my city. I was, moreover, feeling rather excited, because I'd found, in the form of a door in Paris, the way out of my writer's block, and all thanks to that advice from my father, who recommended looking for the hole, however small, that allows us to escape from whatever has us trapped. And suddenly the Breath—yes, the Breath, as Cuadrelli calls that gust of inspiration that always comes from within us, which in itself is its greatest mystery—reminded me that, just as I had done years before actually going to Montevideo, I could visit the website of the Cervantes Hotel, alias the Esplendor, and find out how they were getting on.

It wouldn't be a bad idea, I thought: a flying visit to the source of my obsession with the mystery of Montevideo. Rather than the hotel's website, I opened an article published barely a month earlier in Buenos Aires, which talked about Montevideo and Cortázar and Room 205 of the old Cervantes. It was quite a shock, because one way or another, and I only realized this then, I'd long believed Room 205 to be where I really lived—even when I was miles away from Montevideo—and above all, where I wrote. That's why I reacted as if that article concerned me specifically, when in fact it merely explained that you could now "sleep in the *newly renovated* suite 205 of the old Cervantes Hotel, where the author of *Hopscotch* stayed between November and December of 1954, while taking part in the UNESCO General Conference."

The article included an interview with the new "general manager of what is now the Esplendor by Wyndham Montevideo Cervantes." Not a trace, then, of Manager Mustache, or his assistant, or Nicomedes of Tacuarembó *and other spiders;* a total overhaul. The manager was asked if the sealed door was still there, or had ever been there, and she replied that it wasn't there now, and that she couldn't say for sure if it ever had been, or if it was merely a figment of Cortázar's imagination. One thing she could tell them, the manager went on, was that the door wasn't included in the original plans from 1927, but still, you never knew.

The article made a point of saying that Cortázar's descriptions of what was then the Hotel Cervantes had recently piqued the interest of his loyal readers, lending a permanent aura of mystery to the Esplendor by Wyndham Montevideo Cervantes, despite its recent revamp. And the manager added that anyone who walked the corridors of the hotel would find that the building combined its original 1920s Italian Florentine style with a modern edge: "There's nothing gloomy about it. It has, however, retained its air of calm. This elegant boutique hotel now offers all mod cons, including Room 205, which doesn't have a plaque or anything special on its door. From the outside it looks like any other room, although Cortázar's readers won't see it that way; they'll inevitably think of Petrone, the story's protagonist, an Argentinean man on a business trip. In any case, the current Room 205 of the Esplendor *does not have any hidden doors.*"

The article also explained that the Esplendor boasted

eighty-four refurbished rooms, an indoor heated swimming pool, and a large terrace with views of the lion-colored river, as Cortázar described the Río de la Plata in a letter to the artist Eduardo Jonquières on November 27, 1954. This couldn't have been more astonishing to me, perhaps because for so long I had identified the enigma of Montevideo with that of the universe itself, just as ambiguity had become, for me, the most distinguishing feature of the world we live in.

When someone spends several months writing about a space steeped in mystery, he can end up quite obsessed, and it can therefore come as a terrible shock if another person writes about that same space that is so deeply lodged in his mind. And all the more so if, as had just happened to me, that person's article includes a photo of the "renovated 205," which to my utter amazement showed a room containing neither a sealed door nor a closet but rather a huge sliding door, fashionable white sheets, sunlight pouring in from the street, and most surprising of all, a total area of at least twice as many square feet as that gloomy room where Cortázar had stayed, and where I, too, had spent one restless night, and which I thought I knew by heart, right down to the last detail, to the very last living mygale.

I found it strange to see that whitewashed 205. It was the second time a room in the same hotel had disappeared on me. That, inevitably, was my first thought, before I took another look, hardly believing my eyes, at the photo of the room, so spacious and bright, and devoid of its sealed door.

And I couldn't help remembering how Cortázar, in an interview, had once described spending a night in the hotel: "I don't know who recommended the Hotel Cervantes to me, where there was indeed a poky little room. Between the bed, a table, and a large closet covering a sealed door, there was barely any space left to move."

And on scrutinizing the photo for "the exact place where the fantastical bursts into Cortázar's story," I saw only a modest, unassuming, and very plain light switch. Not knowing quite how to react to that, I thought back to a memory of my mother, who, one morning, having put up with me asking incessantly why the world was so very strange, stopped right there in the middle of Paseo de San Juan and said she was sick and tired of that question and wasn't going to tell me again: the great mystery of the universe was that there should be any mystery to the universe at all.